TASTING DEATH

A VERONICA HOWARD VINTAGE MYSTERY

E. J. GANDOLFO

outsk
p.

Outskirts Press, Inc.
http://www.outskirtspress.com

ISBN: 978-1-9772-3715-6

Author Photo: Shari Nichols Photography.
Cover image created by Outskirts Press, Inc.
© 2021 All rights reserved - used with permission.

Outskirts Press and the "OP" logo are trademarks belonging to Outskirts Press, Inc.

PRINTED IN THE UNITED STATES OF AMERICA

"There is no sincerer love than the love of food."
—George Bernard Shaw

Books by E. J. Gandolfo

To Paint a Murder
A Tale of Deceit
The Tontine Murders
Tasting Death

I dedicate this book to those who make their living, in any capacity, in the food industry.

Chapter 1

Mrs. Violet Thompson was experiencing another sleepless night. The cause of her insomnia was always the same . . . her son Kevin and his group of unsavory friends. He had become selfish and lazy of late, preferring to spend his days at the pool hall instead of looking for another job, and Violet blamed his behavior on their negative influence. After the plant closed down, most of Kevin's coworkers applied at another firm and were immediately hired. He had never bothered to fill out an application and showed no interest in doing so.

Violet knew her son well enough to realize how easily his head was turned by flash and big talk. The truth was that although she and her husband possessed old-fashioned values and a strong work ethic, they had spoiled their only child. The result was that no amount of nagging on her part seemed to make any difference. One day melted into another without any positive changes.

Violet was a widow now and had to watch her spending carefully. Today, she had two housecleaning assignments, both regular customers, and she thanked her lucky stars she was still able to work. Now that Kevin was living back home, her food bill had tripled. Between lending him money that he was in no hurry to pay back, purchasing her weekly lottery tickets, and going to the church bingo every Thursday night, life for Violet Thompson was an ongoing financial challenge.

She stood by the stairs and called to let him know that his breakfast was on the table, gathered her supplies for the day, and walked out to the car, crossing her fingers that it would start up without the usual difficulty.

Violet's first job was at the home of Patricia and Robert Vickers, owners of the upscale Bromfield restaurant, Poppies. In the three years that she had been their cleaning lady, she had never minded working in such a beautiful house. Built in the current 1980s minimalistic contemporary style of concrete and glass, the architectural firm designed it to include all the latest conveniences and innovations. The Vickers had given them a blank check to create a showplace, and they did just that, a one-of-a-kind home that made all who saw it envious.

The house was designed in an open floor plan format, and the centerpiece was a spectacular circular staircase that led the eye up to the cathedral ceiling. Window walls offered sweeping views of a sculpture garden, and the soothing sounds of the waterfall trickling down the north face gave a serene peace and Zen-like tranquility to the property.

The Vickers had invited several friends over for cocktails the night before, so Violet wasn't particularly surprised to see a large mess of glasses and dishes piled up on every available surface. Overflowing ashtrays and empty liquor bottles were scattered everywhere.

She knew from experience that every time the couple entertained, it was to impress, and luckily, the sheer volume of last night's clutter didn't discourage her. She supposed that this party wouldn't be the last one; in fact, it seemed they were hosting even more of these gatherings, each one with more litter to clean up than the previous one. But it was all in a day's work, and Violet couldn't afford to lose a steady job like this one.

Patricia Vickers had left a note on the kitchen table, along with a key to the back door of Poppies, asking her to drive over at 9:00 a.m. sharp and deliver the manila envelope the key was next to. Although the kitchen staff wouldn't be arriving until 10:00 o'clock to start food preparation for the lunch service, the note stressed the importance of Violet leaving the envelope on the butcher block before the restaurant personnel came to work.

When Violet arrived, her car was the only one in the parking lot. She opened the door and looked around, all the while wondering why she had been given this task to perform when there was so much work to do at the house. Once inside, she immediately became aware of how chilly the kitchen was. She put the envelope on the butcher block as directed and turned to leave.

It was then that she noticed that the door to the large walk-in freezer was wide open. She walked over to it and peered inside. What she saw was the body of her employer, Robert Vickers, dead on the floor, his slack mouth and glassy eyes looking very much like the codfish his head was leaning on. Her silent scream propelled her back through the kitchen door as fast as her elderly legs could carry her.

Chapter 2

The morning was crisp and cool, the kind of New England fall weather that makes you glad you're alive. Veronica Howard breathed the air deeply as she waited patiently in front of her Boston brownstone apartment building for her ride to work. Usually, she would drive herself to her store, Veronica's Vintage, located in Bromfield, a small seaside town about fifteen miles north of Boston. Today, her boyfriend, Harry Hunt, was driving because he had to attend a board meeting at the Bromfield Bank and Trust. It was almost impossible to find a parking place in the Back Bay most days, and soon, Harry pulled up in his blue Porsche. She quickly slid into the front seat and arranged her lavender and mauve-pink wool tweed coat and matching skirt around her.

"How's my beautiful girl this morning?" he said, glancing in the rearview mirror.

"All the better for knowing that you're the one who's going to drive," she laughed and kissed his cheek.

He pulled out into the traffic going down Commonwealth Avenue and headed over to the Mystic River Bridge to the North Shore.

Harry and Veronica had been an item for about three years now, and each relished their good fortune at finding each other while firmly entrenched in middle age. They were well matched on many levels, having intelligence, a sense of humor, common sense, and chemistry in common. They were lovers as well as good friends, and both had the wisdom to stay out of the other's space when it was warranted.

They maintained separate residences, and this arrangement worked well for them. They certainly would never consider living without each other, but then again, they could never live together either. And if you asked what the real secret to their successful relationship was, they would both readily admit to falling in love at first sight and respecting the other's privacy.

Veronica was a striking-looking woman with jet-black hair fashionably cut in the bobbed style of the 1920s, with straight bangs and shingled back. Her grass-green eyes were large and reflected her intelligence, and her creamy complexion rarely saw the sun if she could help it. Veronica's elegance, tall stature, and long legs had caught Harry's attention immediately. She often wore the vintage clothes that she sold, and the styles suited her to perfection.

Harry, on the other hand, could easily have been mistaken for a conservative, well-dressed academic. His closely cropped blond hair was just starting to show silver threads, and his tall, thin physique was helped along by several weekly sets on the squash court with friends. He was generally perceived as a wealthy dilettante who managed his family's investments and well-known art collection. He sat on several boards of directors in addition to the Bromfield Bank and

Trust and was an art consultant to museums.

But Harry had another job, one that few of his friends and acquaintances would ever guess he could handle. He was an undercover Special Agent for the Federal Bureau of Investigation. Recruited while he was a Harvard student, his perfect cover was his family's wealth and social position.

The traffic to Bromfield was unusually heavy this morning, and the weatherman's prediction of a clear and sunny October day was turning out to be true. The trees were bathed in the early light, and the leaves were a riot of color in molten gold, flame red, and orange. The town of Bromfield had a maritime history, similar to some of its neighbors, Salem and Marblehead. Veronica fell in love with the place when she was looking for a location for her store. The town square's centerpiece was the original meetinghouse, one of the oldest still in continual use in the United States. The police department and town hall buildings bordered the surrounding green, as did the library and post office, their white-painted facades blending in with the colonial architecture.

Harry dropped Veronica off in front of her store, and she unlocked the door, flipped the closed sign to open, and turned on the lights. She knew foot traffic on Posy Place would become busy soon, and she could already smell the delicious odors coming from the bakery a few doors down. She plugged in the coffeepot in expectation of her daily morning visit from Joe Banks, the jovial and lovable beat cop who regularly took his break at the store. Joe could always be counted on to bring a box of pastries along with the local gossip. Soon, the bell over the front door tinkled, and in he walked.

"Morning, Joe," she chirped and instantly noticed that his usual smile was missing. "Is there something on your mind?" she said.

"Does it show?" he replied.

"I'm afraid it does. Tell me about it."

He selected a lemon Danish and sat down on the blue velvet sofa that hadn't sold yet.

"Well, I've just learned there was a serious assault last night at The Helping Hand soup kitchen. One of the regular volunteers reported that someone attacked him in the men's room and tried to strangle him. He couldn't identify his assailant because he was grabbed from behind, but he struggled and fought him off and reported the incident to one of the permanent staff.

"We've never had any complaints from The Helping Hand," he continued, "and the feeling right now is that one of the patrons may have been high on drugs and needed money. The doorman checks everyone standing in line, but sometimes a troublemaker slips through. It's odd because the victim can't supply any reason why he was targeted."

"I'm sad to hear it too, Joe. You may know I volunteer at the soup kitchen a few nights a month. I hope this won't discourage those who really need a hot meal from going because they might feel they wouldn't be safe."

"There will be a discreet police presence for another week or two. Right now, we think this may have just been a one-time incident by a druggie who got by the doorman."

"Who was attacked? I may know him from one of my shifts."

"Benny Dalton, and apparently he's been a volunteer for some time."

"Benny is one of the chefs and everyone likes him. In fact, I'm scheduled to work with him tomorrow evening."

Chapter 3

The Helping Hand soup kitchen was located in the basement of a former municipal building that the Bromfield town fathers had once decided to close down because of budget constrictions. It was originally built as a private residence by a wealthy shoe factory owner, a pretentious construction of gray quarry stone with carved gargoyles on every corner.

The descendants of the family that built the mansion had made a bequest of their white elephant to the town. The clergy of Bromfield suggested it be converted to a soup kitchen and shelter, and so The Helping Hand became a lifeline to those caught in the economic squeeze.

The shelter upstairs was the smallest part of the building and could house about a dozen people nightly. The soup kitchen occupied the entire basement and typically served an evening meal to about fifty patrons daily, mostly the elderly living on limited pensions, single mothers with young children, and a small group of homeless young men, including a few veterans of the Viet Nam Conflict.

The permanent staff consisted of the director and his

secretary, a pro bono social services counselor, and the head kitchen administrator who occupied the offices in the center of the building. Various organizations and religious groups volunteered daily, and single volunteers, like Veronica, filled in with serving and kitchen duties as needed.

Veronica always looked forward to working there and especially enjoyed chatting to the patrons as they ate, for some, the only meal they would have all day. Aunt Gillian started taking her niece along with her when she volunteered while Veronica was still in her teens. After Gillian died, Veronica continued with the tradition.

Tonight she was assigned to assist in serving the vegetable portion of the meal which consisted of a nourishing soup of white beans and chicory in a tomato broth, a salad of seasonal greens, meat loaf, glazed carrots, mashed potatoes, and a dessert of a slice from the assorted pies and cakes that were donated daily by local restaurants. Meat Loaf Night was always popular, and everyone settled down to eat, the assault on Benny Dalton the chief topic of conversation.

The police had not been able to advance any other theories about why he was victimized, but Benny worked tonight despite still feeling sore from the attack. Veronica saw him talking to another cook, a pleasant woman she knew only as Karen. She waited until there was a lull in the conversation, then walked over to tell him how sorry she was to hear about the assault.

"Thank you, Miss Howard. He took me by surprise and jumped me from behind while I was washing my hands in the men's room. Maybe he thought I had some money on me ... I don't know. But I'm not going to stop volunteering here because of what happened."

"Were you injured at all, Benny?"

"He threw me to the floor, and we struggled. I've got a few cuts and bruises from that. I honestly feel I was not directly targeted but was just in the wrong place at the wrong time. It shouldn't have happened, and that's the bottom line."

Benny then introduced Karen Little to Veronica. "I'm thinking about the safety of Karen here and all the other women volunteers, including you. I just hope everyone becomes vigilant, but not to the point of being paranoid, either."

"I applaud your ability to put it behind you. But if it weren't a random act, do you have any idea why anyone would want to hurt you?"

"I remember only too well when I needed the services of a soup kitchen in my own life and know how important it is to fill both body and soul with food and companionship. I used to be employed as a full-time chef in a fancy, upscale kitchen, but working here with these folks gives me far more satisfaction than when I worked for a greedy restaurant owner."

Veronica silently praised his positive response but was aware that he did not answer her question.

"Where did you work as a chef, Benny?" she asked pointedly.

He hesitated for a few seconds, then answered. "Poppies!" he spat out. "I worked for Robert Vickers and stayed until I couldn't stand it any longer."

The vehemence of his answer surprised her, and she thought a moment before she asked him the question.

"He was murdered recently, wasn't he?"

"Yes, he was," said Benny, "and I'm surprised someone waited so long to do it!" Then he nodded curtly to Veronica and Karen and stalked off to the kitchen.

Karen turned to Veronica with raised eyebrows. "Well," she said, "I guess we know where Benny stands on the subject of Robert Vickers. To tell you the truth, I don't blame him at all for feeling the way he does."

"Did you know Vickers too, Karen?"

"I not only knew him, but I also worked for him as well. Benny isn't overstating the obvious by telling you how awful it was to work for the man. In fact, he fired me a few days after hiring me for not crushing the garlic first before slicing it to give bloom to the flavor. He also didn't care for how I prepared carrots because they weren't cut diagonally, which he considered more pleasing to the eye. After a while, I felt I couldn't do anything right and it affected my work performance, not to mention my ego."

"But didn't he at least give you a chance to do things his way?"

"No, that's just it. The slightest infraction was a big deal. I'm not aware that anyone he ever criticized in that kitchen ever got a second chance. Benny finally got fed up and left shortly after I did."

"Wow," said Veronica. "He sounds like a tyrant."

"His wife, Patricia, hired a cordon bleu-trained chef immediately after we left. I understand he was as temperamental as Robert was, and we were all taking bets about how long he would last. I do miss working with Benny, though. He's a first-class talent; a true artist in the kitchen."

Karen looked over to watch Benny prepare some more side dishes being served at tonight's meal. It didn't escape Veronica's notice that the dreamy look on her face seemed to come from longing as well as from friendship.

"Well, I must get back to the kitchen," she said. "I love vintage clothing and will make a point of coming to your store, Miss Howard. You always look so nice and are a good advertisement for the clothes you sell."

"Thank you, Karen. Please call me Ronnie, and I look forward to seeing you soon."

Chapter 4

The next day, Harry sat in the well-worn chair opposite the desk in the office of Bromfield Police Lieutenant Phil Balducci. Not for the first time, he observed the lieutenant absentmindedly reach for the glass candy jar next to the phone and select a licorice stick, a habit he had developed at the suggestion of his wife to stop himself from smoking cigarettes and the occasional cigar.

The lieutenant had summoned him for a friendly, informal chat between law enforcement officers. The two men enjoyed bouncing ideas off each other. Their friendship had become strong as of late, not only because of their professions and the cases they had worked on together but also because they both held Veronica Howard in high esteem. They continued to address each other formally, a habit that suited them both.

"Any further advancement on the Vickers murder, Lieutenant?" asked Harry, pouring himself a mug of coffee from the pot on the table by the file cabinet.

"Nothing more since it happened. From all appearances, the business is now running in the black. We know that he seemed to have gotten on well with his wife, the pastry chef, who was also his business partner.

"On the down side, he wasn't at all popular with his employees. But then again, if everyone killed the boss they despised, there wouldn't be any restaurants left to eat in."

"Even ex-employees hated Vickers," revealed Harry and recounted what Veronica had learned from Benny Dalton.

"Leave it to your good lady to uncover a hidden story. Looks like we'll have to revisit Mr. Dalton to learn more about his relationship with the ex-boss that he failed to mention he once worked for at Poppies when we interviewed him at The Helping Hand."

"For your ears, Lieutenant," said Harry, leaning over the desk, "the FBI had been keeping an eye on Vickers recently. It seems he may have been involved with drug trafficking, information which has only come to light in the past few days."

Balducci thoughtfully chewed on the licorice stick. "Maybe his restaurant is named Poppies for a reason," he quipped. "I understand Mrs. Vickers will carry on and keep the place open for business."

"Veronica and I have a reservation to eat there this evening. I'll let you know if I see or hear anything out of the ordinary."

"Just don't eat the fish, Mr. Hunt. We found Vickers dead on top of some."

"I'll bear that in mind, Lieutenant, and order a steak."

Chapter 5

One of Veronica's favorite customers, Ada Perkins, who was born and raised in the West End of London, asked if she would be interested in purchasing some vintage clothing that had been handed down in her family. Miss Perkins, a charming elderly spinster, requested a valuation on other family pieces as well.

When Veronica arrived at the small cottage, she was introduced to Ada's friend and cleaning lady, Mrs. Violet Thompson, who was busy dusting the dining room. Over cups of hot tea and homemade scones, the two women discussed the clothing.

"None of my nieces or grandnieces wants these things. The young only want what's in fashion now. I suppose I can't blame them, Ronnie," she sighed. "I probably would feel the same if I were still their age."

"Ada, you'd be surprised at how many young people treasure vintage and antique clothing. They love the novelty of wearing fashions from yesteryear and the quality of the fabric and workmanship. And thank goodness they do because I probably wouldn't own Veronica's Vintage today if that weren't the case."

The pieces Ada showed her were mostly heavy black Victorian wool skirts and white linen tops. A purple satin tea gown with a black lace bodice and bustle was exceptionally nice and had satin shoes to match. Veronica bought everything the old lady had because their condition was excellent, as was their provenance.

While they were talking, Violet walked through the room with a dust rag and was invited to join them.

"Sit down, Violet, and rest your bones. Has Kevin found a job yet?"

"Thanks, Ada," she said and sat down heavily on a needlepoint-covered slipper chair.

"Kevin is my son, Miss Howard, and has been out of work since the plant he worked at closed several months ago. And one of my clients, Mr. Vickers, was murdered last week. It seems like trouble always comes in threes. Oh no," she cried, ticking off the numbers on her fingers, "that's only two. What in the world is coming next?"

"Now, don't go getting your knickers in a twist, dear," admonished Miss Perkins. "Are you still cleaning the Vickers's house?"

"Yes, and thank God I am. She wants me to stay on. I don't mind her so much, although she is kind of fussy. But I don't miss him at all . . . always was in a bad mood . . . forever complaining about something . . . and with all that money!"

She turned to Veronica. "You know, I was the one who found his body, don't you? I can still see him now, dead as a doornail and with the same look on his face as the fish he was on top of.

"Oh," she moaned dramatically, clutching her hair, "what a sight for these old eyes."

"Have a nice cup of tea, dear," urged Ada. "And add a wee drop of whiskey if you fancy it."

"Don't mind if I do," said a now perky Violet, and enthusiastically poured from the decanter on the table.

The three women sat in companionable silence, sipping their tea as the grandfather clock in the hall quietly ticked away the minutes.

"You know, the more I think about it, the more I believe there was something funny going on in that house," Violet said presently, warming to her subject as the liquor loosened her tongue.

"How so, dear?" said Ada, munching on a scone.

"Well, the missus wanted me to run down to the restaurant and hand deliver an envelope when I had a house full of dirty dishes and glassware to clean up after the party they had the night before. She was very clear about when I had to arrive, but the place was empty when I got there. Well, except for Mr. Vickers, of course, who was lying dead in the freezer.

"Oh," she continued, shivering despite herself, "now *that's* something I won't forget in a hurry!"

Violet drained her cup and continued. "And then there was the little packet of sugar I found under the sofa when I was vacuuming the rug. When I showed it to Mrs. Vickers, she snatched it from my hand and told me to forget I had found it.

"I read the papers, you know, and I don't think it was sugar at all," said Violet, wagging her finger at the two women. "Humph. And besides, they weren't even drinking coffee that night, just booze, so there was no need for sugar."

"Have you found any other little packets?" said Veronica, her curiosity now piqued.

"No, but I did find a gun. It was in a big wooden box at the back of the hall closet that I had to move when I was cleaning, along with a stack of money. It's a good thing that I'm an honest woman, but there's no denying I could use a little extra help that way, especially now that my Kevin is back living with me and eating me out of house and home."

"Did you mention any of this to Mrs. Vickers, by any chance?" said Veronica.

"No, I did not. My lips are sealed and zippered," she said firmly, making a little twist motion with her fingers over her mouth.

Veronica smiled. It seemed that the zipper had come undone after a few sips of boozy tea.

Chapter 6

Harry arrived at the store after his visit with Lieutenant Balducci in time to take Veronica to lunch. They decided to try the new burger restaurant that had just opened at the other end of Posy Place. As they strolled down the picturesque and charming street, breathing in the crisp and fresh early-autumn air, Veronica was happy that she never had cause to regret renting a store here. The buildings always reminded her of a picturesque Victorian English village.

"Best time to live in New England," said Harry, admiring the colorful arrangements of gold- and bronze-colored chrysanthemums planted in the window boxes along the length of the street.

"Except maybe for spring," added Veronica, as they walked arm and arm. Her vintage outfit of a red and black plaid wool knitted cape with a hood that she wore with black patent leather boots provided a fashionable contrast to his traditional Brooks Brothers camel hair coat with a brown velvet collar.

Bob's Burgers was an unpretentious little place already busy with the lunch crowd. They found an empty table in the back and read the menu.

"I think I'll have a hamburger," announced Harry.

"Good choice, Einstein, since that's all they serve here," teased Veronica.

"Hey, wait a minute," he said with mock indignation. "They also have some healthy options, too: veggie burgers, soy burgers, and nut burgers." He pointed to a chalkboard menu on the wall listing today's specials for emphasis.

"I'm not your girlfriend for nothing, Harry Hunt," she said, wagging a finger in his direction. "The day you eat a burger that's not made with red meat is the day I fall off this chair."

He laughed and gave his order to the waitress. When she delivered the plate, it contained a double beef patty cheeseburger on a seeded roll with bacon, lettuce, tomato, dill pickles, sautéed mushrooms, and roasted red peppers. He managed to bite into the mound, chewed thoughtfully, and pronounced it to be very good indeed.

"Don't forget we're having dinner at Poppies tonight."

Harry groaned. "Maybe I'll just order a salad."

"I won't hold my breath until you do," replied Veronica and slapped him playfully with her napkin.

While they were eating, she recapped her visit with Ada Perkins and Violet Thompson. It seemed that the Vickers had a lot more going on than just a cocktail party. Harry mentioned his conversation with the lieutenant and the possible drug connection.

When Veronica told him about Violet Thompson's discovery of drugs, a gun, and money, Harry raised an eyebrow.

"Balducci never mentioned this, and I doubt the police

have any idea these items were in the house before they searched. I think we should inform him after we finish eating."

The table next to them became free, and two men in jeans and plaid shirts sat down. One had more salt than pepper in his hair and appeared to be in his late 40s. His companion was younger and had sandy-blond hair. Their voices carried to the adjoining table despite their effort to speak softly.

"When's the next shipment?" asked the sandy-haired man.

His companion looked around before answering. "The stuff's coming in on the plane tonight. I'll be there to help unload, and so will you."

"I got people lined up to buy," said Sandy Hair. "Can I get any of it tonight?"

"We gotta deliver it to the restaurant first. The boss needs to check it before it hits the street. You know how this works by now, Kevin."

"Yeah, well, all I know is that I lose money every hour I can't sell it," he whined.

Veronica's napkin dropped to the floor, and she slowly leaned down to pick it up. Harry started to speak, but she motioned to him with her other hand to be quiet.

"You just handle your end, Kevin, and don't worry 'bout nothin' else. Vee will pay you your cut from the last shipment tonight. Just be on time. She's the boss now, so take my advice. Don't be an ass and try to cross her."

The two men sat in sullen silence, ate quickly, then left.

Harry and Veronica stared at each other. She immediately filled him in on the conversation that she was able to hear. Ordinarily, if anyone else were recounting a disjointed discussion between two strangers overheard in a noisy restaurant and thought it important, he would laugh.

However, the coincidence of the names mentioned made it significant and soon they found themselves sitting in front of Lieutenant Balducci recounting the tale. He sat with his arms folded across his chest and listened carefully to what they were saying.

"Well, now, isn't that interesting," he said presently and pressed the intercom button on his phone. His sergeant came into the office.

"Anderson, run the name Kevin Thompson and see what you get. Also, Miss Howard has it on good authority that the party the Vickers had the night before Robert Vickers was murdered was most likely fueled by cocaine or heroin, or both. Get me a list of the guests if you can."

He turned to Veronica. "How did you put one and one together, Miss Howard? I mean, when did you first make a connection that these two men may have had anything to do with the Vickers investigation?"

"I only had to look at the man, Kevin, Lieutenant. He's the spitting image of his mother, whom I had only just met this morning. She complained that her son Kevin was out of work and was mooching off her and not bothering to look for another job.

"You see," she continued, "Mrs. Thompson regularly cleans the Vickers's house. She said she found a packet of drugs that she first thought was sugar under a piece of furniture, and Mrs. Vickers told her to forget she had ever seen it, which made her suspicious. And Mrs. Thompson also found the body of Robert Vickers, as you know, so there's another connection.

"And then let's not forget about a box of money, along with a gun hidden in a closet at the house that she also stumbled on to but was evidently taken out of the closet before you arrived to search the place."

The two men stared at each other.

"Does she do this all the time, Mr. Hunt?" asked Balducci in wonder.

"Enough so that you can't discount any of this information, Lieutenant."

"Boys, boys," giggled Veronica, shrugging her shoulders, "it's not all just luck, you know. I got a chill down my spine—my 'second sight' kicking in—alerting me to watch out, that's all."

"Are you sure it wasn't just indigestion from your lunch?" quipped Balducci.

They all laughed, but Veronica knew she was right. She was born with a caul across her face, a thin membrane known as the Veil of St. Veronica that folklore said was supposed to give her the power of second sight. All her life, she had the uncanny ability to know when something dangerous or significant would happen, and that special gift had saved her life on more than one occasion.

"Well, all we have to do now is prove this supposition," said the lieutenant.

"Veronica and I are having dinner tonight at Poppies, as I told you. We'll keep our eyes and ears open as civilians eating a nice dinner and let you know if there are any developments."

But their dinner had to be postponed at the last minute to the following night. A call from FBI headquarters summoned Harry to a hastily called evening meeting regarding the recent epidemic of drug distribution and drug-related deaths on the North Shore of Boston. His attendance was mandatory.

Chapter 7

The municipal airport in Danvers, the town next to Bromfield, accommodated mostly single-owner aircraft and small corporate jets that were housed in five hangers. The usual aviation services were available, and six mechanics worked full time at the field. A little café on-site served beverages, sandwiches, and soups and opened early, around 5:00 a.m. and closed promptly at 3:00 in the afternoon, when traffic and business started to slow down.

A twin-engine, fixed-wing Beech Baron came down in a soft landing around midnight and taxied over to the east side of the field, coming to rest on a neglected portion of tarmac partially overgrown with weeds some way from the runway. The pilot deplaned, put chocks behind the wheels, and turned to greet the two men who had been waiting in the parking lot for his arrival.

They shook hands, then proceeded to unload the cargo of large boxes with condensation on them and stamped "refrigeration required."

The night was clear and breezy and the wind sock flapped intermittently from its pole as the men worked quickly to

transfer the boxes to their rented cube van. The whole proce-
dure took less than fifteen minutes. The only eyes taking in
the scene belonged to a coyote peering out from the tall grass
that formed the perimeter of this part of the field.

The van was soon on its way to Poppies Restaurant,
which would usually be closed at this hour. The van circled
the parking lot, and the two drivers made sure there were no
stragglers in the vicinity to notice them unloading. Kevin
Thompson got out of the truck and knocked three times on
the door to the kitchen entrance.

A worker came out, glanced around the parking lot, and
propped open the door. The cargo was moved swiftly indoors
and stacked in the walk-in freezer, all except the boxes with a
red seal discreetly affixed to the upper left-hand corner. Those
were placed on the butcher block and carefully opened, one
by one.

Patricia Vickers, wearing protective yellow rubber gloves,
saw to this part of the consignment herself. She carefully
lifted the contents onto the wood block and stepped back.
The still-frozen fish would have to thaw out a bit longer before she could insert her hand into each gaping mouth and
extract the small packet of white powder that was stuffed
inside.

She peeled off her gloves and turned to the two men.
"Well, boys, any trouble to report?"

Salt-And-Pepper Hair said "no," and Kevin Thompson
did the same.

"Good," she said. "That's what I like to hear. Help yourselves to a beer while we wait for the fish to defrost."

It didn't take long before the drug packets could be

extracted and stored away in the hidden safe in the office. Patricia sat down at her desk, opened her record book, and ran her finger down the column of figures.

"Well, Kevin, it looks like I owe you seven fifty from last week's take. Any problems I should know about?"

"I can sell more, like I told you. Word's around the stuff is available." He sniffed and rubbed his nose on the sleeve of his jacket several times.

Patricia stared at him, then placed a stack of bills on the desk.

"I hope you're not sampling the goods, Kevin, because if you are, that will make you sloppy and careless. And I will be short of product, and then I won't be happy." She uttered her words ominously, quiet and precise, and her eyes were cold black slits, like a cobra sizing up its prey while waiting to strike.

"Naw, I don't touch the stuff. I'm just allergic to shellfish, that's all. You probably got lots of that around here, right?"

"Of course I have shellfish here. It's a restaurant, after all. But you usually have to eat it first before any allergy symptoms show up."

"Not me. All I have to do is just be around the stuff. Anyway, I already told you. I don't use drugs. I just wanna make more money, that's all," he whined. "I got plans."

"I just hope your plans don't conflict with mine," she said. "For now, we will continue with the schedule. If you have a problem with that, let me know, and I'll make other arrangements."

"I'm cool, Mrs. Vee. I'm cool. You can count on me."

She handed him the cash. "I hope so, Kevin," she warned. "I don't like ugly surprises."

Chapter 8

Patricia Vickers was handling her new status as a widow quite well. As an equal partner and one-half owner of a successful restaurant, she had been very familiar with her husband's idiosyncrasies. She had learned a long time ago that playing second fiddle to an egotist wasn't really so bad, as long as you included some of the better perks.

She met her then-future husband at culinary school where they had both enrolled when they were in their early twenties. He found he was more suited to running the front of the house and the kitchen staff than actually cooking. Her specialty was desserts, and she was an excellent and inventive pastry chef.

Patricia and Robert dated steadily while attending school, and she was quite surprised when he announced his intention of opening an upscale restaurant only a few months after they graduated. She knew Robert came from a wealthy family and that he had long been considered to be the black sheep. He expected to come into a large inheritance on his twenty-third birthday, and when he proposed to her, she happily accepted.

They solidified their marriage by working together every day in a professional kitchen. Their arrangement wouldn't have suited every couple, but Patricia grew used to him barking orders because she was secure in her own abilities. He knew her skills were a major draw to their business, and he gave her free reign to hire an assistant baker.

Despite his ego and maybe because of it, Robert and Patricia were a successful team. Soon, Poppies became the premier gastronomic destination for affluent diners who wanted to be seen. But mostly they wanted to eat well, no matter the cost. The Vickers had the funds to hire a top cordon bleu chef, and the menu now embraced the currently popular nouvelle cuisine aesthetic.

Unfortunately, Robert had developed a gambling habit along the way that quickly got out of control. His trips to the casinos in Atlantic City and Las Vegas became more frequent, but the cards were not particularly kind to him lately.

The young couple's beautiful contemporary, custom-designed home had cost quite a bit more than they planned on spending. They wanted a show house, and they got it, and when they entertained, money was no object. It went without saying that the food and drink at their parties were superb, but the added expense of offering their guests high-quality cocaine to keep up with their growing reputation as the hosts to beat was starting to take its toll.

One day, Robert met a friend of a friend who made him an offer that appeared to come just in time. Some outstanding restaurant invoices needed to be paid promptly and, for the Vickers to keep their good name from being tarnished in their industry, the offer had to be seriously considered.

It was now too late for Robert to rethink his gambling habit, and most of the money from his inheritance had already been spent. His gambling addiction and now the added vice of drugs that he had developed a regular taste for could mean risking serious jail time, hefty fines, or both. However, the money they would make in dealing drugs would put them back on top of their world. The decision was made, and now, it was time for them to take action.

They were at home, arguing loudly.

"I don't like what you're telling me, Robert. We've spent a lot of time and trouble building up the business and have sunk everything into Poppies, only to have you now fritter away the profits."

"If it weren't for my inheritance, Patty, we wouldn't have been able to get where we are. *I'm* the driving force behind Poppies, and don't you forget it," he yelled.

"Oh, you don't let me forget it for a minute. And now, we're forced into the position of having to become drug dealers just to keep the doors open!"

"I've already told you, I can quit gambling any time I want."

"Save it because I've heard it all before, Robert. And now, it's too late."

She stood up and tried to stop him from leaving the room, but he shoved her roughly out of the way.

This action would have been unthinkable even a year ago, but now that he was also using cocaine regularly, he had become emboldened. She tried it too but it was not to her taste. The truth was that none of Robert's vices was to her liking.

Patricia was the kind of woman who wanted to be always in control of her emotions and reasoned that one of them had to stand firm and see that their business's profits didn't disappear up his nose or at the casinos. Even she realized she couldn't keep a twenty-four-hour watch on her husband as his bad habits were definitely getting the best of him.

One day, their accountant came to her with some figures that frightened her. Robert had always been in charge of the financial end of things, but she had no idea they were on such thin ice. The answer became immediately apparent to her: they had to risk becoming drug dealers regardless of whether she liked it.

Patricia demanded that Robert stop going to the casinos until they could pay their bills and vendors. Even he knew they could lose everything and grudgingly agreed to stop. But the reality of stopping soon became abhorrent to him, and he had no intention of giving up what had now taken over his life. It was as if he were a completely different man. His choices were terrible, and he couldn't avoid the continuing downward spiral that his life had become.

Chapter 9

The drug lord operating in the Greater Bromfield area in the early 1980s was based in Boston. He was a well-spoken, dapper gentleman who wore five-hundred-dollar custom-made suits, handmade Italian leather shoes, and smoked Cuban cigars. His preferred mode of transportation was a chauffeur-driven black Cadillac limousine, and he always traveled with two men who could only be best described as enforcers without a conscience. The major difference between this drug lord and the rest of his numbers operating in other parts of the country was that he had an Ivy League college education and a law degree.

Aldo Silvio was the new breed of drug entrepreneur, and he was anxious to sell his product to the well-to-do in addition to the street trade. He knew that this upmarket clientele would purchase with alarming regularity. He also reasoned that the ideal distribution conduit for his operation would be to smuggle it in the mouths of freshly caught fish packed in ice on the boats of the fleets he owned and controlled. The fish were delivered to the hand-picked restaurants that he also controlled, and the drugs were distributed through dealers to the regular channels.

This arrangement worked perfectly for the Vickers, and Poppies had now become the perfect cover for the distribution of drugs in the Bromfield area. Their cut of the profits kept the doors open, but instead of being happy with this arrangement, Robert was now becoming more sullen than usual. His gambling habit was spinning out of control, even though he had promised Patricia he would give it up.

Robert's anger at his now-regular losses resulted in him regularly intimidating the staff. He even started to bully the French chef, a man consumed by his own self-importance and who possessed a very similar temperament to Robert's. One day, their personalities clashed in a serious confrontation, and, in a fit of anger, Chef tore off his white toque and jacket, threw them on the floor, yelled, "I quit," and stomped out the door.

Patricia realized she had to act quickly and immediately offered the top job to the sous chef, Benny Dalton, who was both talented and laid-back, to step in to take his place. Everyone liked and respected Benny, and it did not pass unnoticed that he was not given to hysterical temper tantrums like his recently departed predecessor.

If Robert stayed out of the kitchen, working at Poppies was tolerable for everyone. Benny was given a substantial raise. Now, the former homeless man with poor prospects was suddenly the head chef in a top-rated restaurant. For the present, work returned to normal.

Bennett Dalton had started life as the only son in a family of college professors of comfortable means who had inherited some family money. His parents were well respected professionals and couldn't understand why their intelligent second child had no interest in following in their footsteps and teach. Benny's instinct to go his own way manifested itself early. He had always been a headstrong child who could never be coerced into doing something he did not want to do. Instead of enrolling in college, he joined the marines and was immediately deployed to Viet Nam, much to his parents' dismay. What Benny saw and experienced there molded him into a man who could not be pushed around.

Tall, handsome, and blessed with a full head of curly, thick, black hair, Benny's turquoise-blue eyes and perpetual sexy pout broke more than a few female hearts. He was clever and witty when he wanted to be, but he also possessed a short fuse, and he did not suffer fools gladly.

After his military discharge, he enrolled in culinary school and found his calling. He loved to experiment with spices and tastes that lingered on the palate. He had found a profession that suited his adventurous and creative spirit. The fact that his choice of career made his parents furious was all the better for him.

Benny's first job was as an assistant to a chef/owner of a small Greek restaurant. The man was older and had spent his entire life in a professional kitchen. He saw something in the young man that reminded him of himself when he was Benny's age and took him under his wing, teaching him all he knew about running a kitchen for profit. He shared his family's recipes and secret spice mixes and taught Benny how to listen to his customers' likes and dislikes.

The man's family did not want any part of their father's business, but despite their feelings, when the old man announced his intention to sell to Benny, they became belligerent and nasty. The two sons, especially, one a physician and the other an accountant, did not want a stranger taking over the family business. It was of no consequence to them that their expensive education was paid for with their father's sweat and toil; they just didn't want a nonfamily member to profit. They were outraged that their father had not consulted them before he made his decision.

One day, the old man had a severe stroke. Benny visited him in the hospital and realized he could never return to work. He was stunned to learn that his friend and mentor had signed a paper giving him total proprietorship, and the old man's lawyer assured Benny that everything was upfront and legal. When he died a week later, Benny felt a deep and overwhelming sadness for the man who had always treated him with kindness.

Out of respect, he decided to keep the restaurant's name the same, Vasilaki's, "Little William" in Greek. Benny was overjoyed at his good fortune and worked on updating the business out of his own pocket while keeping the menu almost the same. He spent almost every penny he had on new construction and expanded seating.

It wasn't long before the family tried to take over ownership. Their lawyers had discovered a loophole in the contract, and they came to Benny with a proposition. They would assume ownership and continue to pay Bennie a salary, but he had to seek approval from them before changing anything in the restaurant or on the menu.

He turned down their proposal and found himself heavily in debt and homeless almost overnight. Depressed and at the end of his rope, Benny found himself taking his meals at The Helping Hand soup kitchen. He refused to use the upstairs shelter and slept at friends' apartments when he wasn't drinking. Turning to his family for help was not an option. His drinking finally got the best of him, and even his loyal friends would no longer offer him a couch to sleep on. The shelter and soup kitchen became a lifeline to the proud man.

One day, he overheard a staff member discussing plans for a retirement party for one of the volunteer chefs. Benny approached the director, Mr. Jones, and asked him if he could volunteer and take his place. When Jones hesitated, Benny came up with a brilliant idea. He suggested the man taste a meal that he would cook for him right on the spot using the kitchen ingredients. It was lunchtime, the man was hungry, and they were the only two there.

Jones reluctantly agreed, sat down, and watched Benny carefully as he walked over to inspect the contents of the cabinets and the refrigerator. Soon, pots and pans were heating up, and it was clear that Benny Dalton knew what he was doing. He produced a delicious, gourmet-quality, three-course meal just using the donated and simple basic ingredients on hand in less than twenty minutes.

The director was amazed and asked Benny to sit down and give him a verbal résumé of his work experience. He listened carefully.

Presently, he replied, "Well, Mr. Dalton, what can I say? You certainly know how to cook, and it isn't often we have volunteer chefs who have culinary school experience."

"I can do this, Mr. Jones. Just give me a chance. I've been coming here to eat for awhile, and right now I'm down on my luck. I just need an opportunity."

Jones thought a minute. "If you promise to show up when you're supposed to, give up drinking, and prove to me you can go the distance, I'll let you volunteer here. You can continue to sleep upstairs, I insist on that, and if you work well with the others, then I'll say yes."

Benny fulfilled all that was asked of him. He knew he couldn't throw away this chance. One morning, Mr. Jones came into the kitchen while Benny organized the evening meal and asked him to sit down. The look of alarm on Benny's face was immediate.

"Is everything all right? Are you happy with me so far?"

"As you know, your work here is voluntary. I can't pay you, Benny, and believe me, I wish I could. But I have a proposition for you. A friend of mine owns a restaurant nearby and needs an assistant chef. I have explained your circumstances and your capabilities to him, and he's willing to give you a chance. It's not a fancy place, but it's a steady job, and he will pay you the going rate."

Benny was speechless. This kind gesture could not have come at a more crucial time for him.

"I don't know what to say, Mr. Jones. I'm grateful to you for offering me this chance."

"Please call me Brad. What you don't know about me is that I was practically a broken man myself when I returned from Viet Nam. That conflict stays with me daily, and I know you experience it as well. I was pretty much in the same boat as you before someone took me under their wing and straightened me out.

"I returned to college and got my degree, and here I am today. I see a lot of me in you, Benny. I know you can come back too, and I have faith that you will."

The two men shook hands. "I won't let you down, Brad. Believe me; I won't let you down."

Benny didn't let Brad Jones down or his new employer. He worked at the restaurant for a year and continued to volunteer at The Helping Hand. He was able to save money and rent a small apartment in Bromfield. When the time came to move on from the restaurant, he left, knowing he had done his best for his friend, the owner, and himself.

He answered an advertisement for a sous chef job at Poppies and was hired by Robert Vickers. He had heard the rumors about how difficult Vickers could be, but working in a top-rated restaurant had been his goal. He decided to concentrate on his future and overlook the owner's overbearing personality. He gritted his teeth and carried on, but there were days when he thought he could gladly murder his boss.

Chapter 10

One day, as Patricia was walking through the dining room after the lunch service, she happened to glance over and saw a dapper-looking man sitting alone at a corner table. She realized it was Aldo Silvio and hurried over to pay her respects. He saw her approach and put down the menu he was reading.

"Ah, Mrs. Vickers, what do you recommend I order for lunch?"

"Why didn't you phone ahead and tell me you were coming, Mr. Silvio?" she asked, shaking his proffered hand. "I could have arranged something special." She snapped her fingers to a passing waiter for the wine list.

"But then I wouldn't have been able to surprise you," he said.

Patricia realized she was being evaluated. His steady stare told her that. Robert had always been the liaison for the drug business, and she had a strong feeling that changes were going to be made as of today.

"Then allow me the honor to cook you a delicious lunch and dessert."

"I look forward to it, my dear, but it's you I wish to speak with. Let me enjoy the food, wine, and atmosphere, and we will talk later, just the two of us."

She realized his words were a command. She hurried back to the kitchen and told Benny to immediately prepare his specialty, Lobster Thermidor, which was not on the menu that day. Her hands were shaking as she assembled an apple tart, and her thoughts were swirling with what this powerful and dangerous man had on his mind.

She knew that Robert had dropped the ball, that his vices had gotten in the way of any advancement in both their business and personal life. Before he died, he had turned into a pathetic shell, propped up by her and her ambition to keep their dreams alive.

Patricia was also aware that if Mr. Silvio had wanted her dead, he only had to snap his fingers. She knew Robert was murdered for a reason, and the manner of his death was a clear sign that he had breached some kind of code.

As Patricia kneaded and rolled out the pastry dough, her mind became calm again, the familiar motions of her profession putting her at ease. The smell of sugar and butter to her was like the scent of Chanel No. 5 to other women. She knew the power that cooking and baking had on some people and reasoned, in her present, calm state, that Mr. Silvio was probably a passionate and sensuous man. He could be won over by a provocative woman who could satisfy all of his senses. She would present him with a delightful dessert—after all, he was a hungry man—then she would listen to what he had to say.

Benny outdid himself with his Lobster Thermidor dish,

and the smile on Mr. Silvio's face reflected his enjoyment of the effort. The rich sherry and butter sauce was subtle and delicious, and the lobster meat was sweet with the fresh taste of the sea. The accompanying arugula salad was simply dressed with oil and vinegar with a dash of thyme, and the wine pairing was perfect. Silvio asked to see the chef, and when Benny presented himself at his table, Silvio shook his hand.

Patricia soon followed with her plate and watched with delight as he tucked into her creation.

"Congratulations, my dear. Your pastry is as light as air, and the balance of sweetness against the tart apple is superb."

She let out an audible sigh. She knew now that she could deal with this man. He understood her passion, and she now understood his.

Chapter 11

Patricia led Mr. Silvio into her office and closed the door. Robert had installed soundproof baize fabric to cover the office door and walls when they built the restaurant to block out the noises of a professional kitchen while they were trying to do their book work. The room was large and had a sofa that converted into a bed along one wall so she could rest after a long day.

Mr. Silvio walked over and sat next to her, and she waited for him to speak, all the while observing his expensive attire and elegant and expressive hands and perfectly manicured nails.

"I'm aware of certain, shall we say, irregularities, in your business lately, Mrs. Vickers, and I want to reassure you that I'm here to help."

She looked down demurely at her folded hands resting in her lap. "Please, call me Patricia," she said quietly.

"Patrizia," he said softly, giving an extra vowel to the Italian pronunciation of her name. It rolled off his tongue like a poem.

"Patrizia, you must realize that I always understand what

happens in the businesses that I am involved with. I was aware that Robert had become a liability. What you have to decide now is how you feel about the outcome."

She looked up and met his eyes. "It hurt me that he had sunk so low, Mr. Silvio, but please understand that I want to continue our distribution arrangement with you, and nothing will get in the way of that. I need the money to keep this restaurant afloat. I want that more than anything."

He took her hand gently in his and said nothing for a while. Presently, he asked, "Did you love your husband, Patrizia?"

"He let me down."

He squeezed her hand a little harder and asked again, "Did you *love* him?"

It took her some time before she answered, but she knew what she had to say.

"Not for a long time; certainly not at the end," she whispered finally. "He was no longer the man I married, and his insatiable taste for gambling and drugs made him into a complete stranger."

"Then leave it to me. The restaurant will continue as before, and all bills will be taken care of. I will become your silent partner, and you will be in charge of your dream. I understand that you are a passionate woman and you had been thwarted by a weak man. Make your peace with that and move on with my help and guidance."

"I don't know what else to say, Mr. Silvio, but thank you."

"Call me Aldo, my dear. We will make a good team."

He leaned over and took her face in his hands and gently kissed her mouth. The warmth of his breath and the scent of his cologne intoxicated her. She returned his kiss with more ardor than she expected, the possibilities of this new situation becoming clear now. This man had sealed Robert's fate with the snap of his fingers, and she knew her life would change for the better if she aligned it to his.

"Did you have Robert killed?" she whispered.

"He disappointed me, Patrizia, and I so dislike being disappointed."

She finally knew the truth.

"I won't ever disappoint you, Aldo," she said, and her breath left her in a heavy sigh.

Chapter 12

Benny was sitting at the small desk in the corner of the kitchen, writing a list of instructions to give to his assistant for the dinner service. But at the same time, he was also observing the closed door to the office. He had seen Patricia and this customer, who complimented him on his food, walk in and wondered who he was and why she was so deferential to him.

Benny realized that he was attracted to Patricia. They had a mutual bond, and she understood the food business and wanted to make the best of their shared profession. They were both perfectionists and realized that perfection was what gave them job satisfaction.

Another part of him was attracted to her quiet and calm demeanor. He knew sometimes she could be tough; he saw it when Robert wasn't holding up his end. However, she handled her errant husband with kid gloves, and Benny knew it was better for her to try to coax him than to yell at him. If it were up to him, Robert would have been the recipient of a good beating, which was no more than he deserved, and that he himself would have been more than happy to deliver the beating.

He was also attracted to her pretty face and slim figure. She usually wore jeans in the kitchen along with her starched white chef's jacket and comfortable clogs, her long blond hair wound up in a haphazard knot on top of her head and held in place with a clip. She was lovely without wearing a lot of makeup. Her clear complexion and the rosy glow of her skin when she took pastry from the hot oven gave her a youthful look even though she was well past the first flush of youth.

Benny also knew from experience how unwise it was to start a relationship where you worked, especially not with the married half of the couple who employed you. Of course, he never had any trouble attracting the opposite sex. Sometimes when he and Patricia were working on opposite sides of the kitchen during the same shift, they would joke and laugh together, talking loudly over the clatter of the pots and pans. They could almost communicate telepathically with just a glance.

When Robert was alive and in the office shouting over the phone if the door was open or he was in one of his usual bad moods, Benny just ignored him and got on with his work. At least Robert realized that if Benny was going to stay in his employ, he had to keep his nose out of the kitchen. Patricia, on the other hand, was the person Benny preferred to deal with anyway. They had always lightly flirted with each other, which was fine with Benny. It never seemed to upset Robert. In fact, Benny was sure that Robert never noticed, and he wondered what kind of marriage they really had.

Presently, the door opened, and the prosperous-looking man walked out, waving to Benny as he exited through the kitchen to the main dining room of the restaurant. Benny's eyes followed him, and it was then that he noticed the waiting limousine with driver and bodyguard outside the front door.

Patricia soon appeared, winding up her disheveled long blond hair with one hand while attaching a hair clip with the other. Her face was flushed, and her eyes were shining. Suddenly, the situation became clear. Someone had replaced her husband in her affections . . . and it wasn't him.

Chapter 13

Diane Andrews stopped by Veronica's Vintage to see her friend. They had shared several adventures and kept in touch regularly since Diane had been named head librarian at the Bromfield Public Library. They had both discovered the body of her late ex-husband, who had been killed while they were investigating a ring of art thieves. Diane had turned her life around by going back to college to get her degree and was very happy with the new man in her life, a local fishing boat captain who adored her.

Veronica looked up from her desk as Diane walked in.

"Well, hello. You're looking particularly well and pleased today."

"I want to make a special purchase, Ronnie. Peter has proposed, and I've accepted. He wanted to buy me an engagement ring at the local jewelry store chain, but I anticipated that and asked him if he would mind if I chose one myself, with his approval, of course."

Ronnie rushed over and hugged her friend. "I'm so happy for you, Diane. You deserve a good man, and you've finally found him."

"I have to pinch myself when I realize this is really happening. After my horrible marriage to Carl, it's almost as if my life now is a dream. And what I've been dreaming about is a certain ring in your jewelry case." She walked over and pointed to an antique diamond ring from the Victorian era. It was platinum with a filigree oval top set with a large old mine-cut stone, flanked with two smaller baguette-cut sapphires.

Veronica reached in the case and placed the ring on a velvet pad. Diane took off her coat, put her shoulder bag on the floor, and sat down.

"Susan," she called to her assistant, "would you please pour Mrs. Andrews a cup of coffee. She's doing some serious shopping over here."

They laughed, and Diane slipped the ring on her finger, moving her hand around to watch the diamond catch the light. "Ooh, it's so beautiful, Ronnie."

"And it fits!" exclaimed Veronica.

Susan came over with the coffee and admired the ring. "Don't you want to try on any others, Mrs. Andrews?" she asked, placing the cup and saucer on the counter.

"Nope; no need," exclaimed Diane. "This is the one. Tell me about it, Ronnie."

"It's from the 1890s, and I obtained it from an estate in Boston. The center stone weighs a little over one karat and is eye clean, with no inclusions. The color is excellent. In fact, if you take the ring off for a minute, I'll show you the name of the very famous store in New York that it was originally purchased from, which is stamped on the inside of the shank."

"You will have to pry it from my finger first," exclaimed Diane. They all laughed. "My next question is, will Peter be able to afford it?"

Veronica consulted a small black book on her desk. She walked back and whispered a figure in Diane's ear, who gasped when she heard it.

"But can you sell it for that price? I mean, will you make a profit?"

"Diane," she said with feeling, "you are my dear friend, and you have fallen in love twice: once with a wonderful man and again with a fabulous ring that looks as if it were made for you. It is a fine example of an antique diamond ring from a famous maker, and I can't think of any other person who should be wearing it."

Diane jumped up from the chair and hugged Veronica. "I'll call Peter as soon as I get back to the library, and he'll be in to buy it later this afternoon. There will be no need for me to act surprised. He said he just wants me to be happy, and I am so very happy. I've always dreamed of owning a beautiful antique ring like this, and now I have it."

Diane twirled around, holding her hand up to the light. "I feel just like Princess Diana, right now. Sure, her ring is bigger, but she couldn't be any happier than I am at this very moment." She reached into her handbag for a hanky, and both women became misty-eyed.

"Harry and I are having dinner tonight at Poppies. Please, you and Peter come with us as our guests so we can all celebrate your engagement."

Diane wagged her head up and down and started to cry. "I will have to give the ring back to you now so he can present it to me properly later."

"Meet us at Poppies at seven, and we'll all have a wonderful, happy evening."

Chapter 14

The port of Gloucester, a neighboring city about ten miles from Bromfield, had always been an important fishing center. After more than two hundred years, the industry was still a major employer in the area. Generations of families made their living hauling their catches from their boats to plants for processing. Mr. Silvio was well known along the waterfront. His boats and crews were always working, even during the current economic slump due to government regulations and competition from foreign vessels fishing in the same waters.

Huge tuna processing boats from Japan and Russia were fishing just beyond the international three-mile limit, too close to the Atlantic coast shoreline, depleting the stock and making it more difficult for local fishermen to compete. Generations of families who had always fished in these waters had to appeal to their government representatives to do something about their plight. Help was slow in coming, and it became clear to some that they had to resort to other means to keep their boats working regularly.

Most of the old-time fishing families of Gloucester

were of Sicilian, Greek, and Portuguese descent, with some younger workers with Irish roots. When the boats returned after weeks at sea, some venturing up as far as the Grand Banks, the bars in town did a rush business. Stories were traded, business was conducted, repairs and maintenance on the boats were performed, bank loans were repaid, and new crews were signed up for the next trip. Boredom was usually alleviated with copious alcohol consumption.

Life at sea was mostly a generational occupation. Fathers, sons, and grandsons passed down their stories and adventures, and not one of them could picture themselves in any other job. The cult of the New England fisherman meant always having the smell of the sea in your nostrils and forever longing to leave the safety of dry land for the roll of the waves under your feet, to belong to a brotherhood of men who did battle with the elements every time a boat left the harbor.

Often they were lucky, but Mother Nature could turn on a dime. The graveyards were full of men who were claimed by the very sea they couldn't get enough of, the stone slabs engraved with the names of those who rested at the bottom of the ocean and not in the grassy land they were brought up on.

In the end, it was every man working in tandem with his brother hauling in the catch that would keep them in funds until the next tour. No one else could ever really understand the life; the thrill of man against nature, the ongoing fight against time, and the satisfaction that came from conquering the creatures that lived in the deep . . . Fishing for these men was as much of a calling as it was just a job.

It was well known that Mr. Silvio's crew was paid higher wages, and if you were fortunate enough to be signed on to one of his boats, you knew you had to shut your mouth, do your work, and never complain.

It was rumored that the circuit his drug trade took started with the loading of the refined cocaine from the fields of South America that was then transferred to small planes that flew the product to southern Nova Scotia. The drugs were air dropped in parcels next to the fishing boats he owned and loaded on board. Eventually, the small packets of powder were stuffed into the cavities of the freshly caught fish that were destined for the port cities along the New England coast, most notably Gloucester, Mass.

This morning, Aldo Silvio was sitting in his office at the Santa Flavia Fisheries in Gloucester, a large and modern warehouse located along the waterfront docks. It was furnished in an unpretentious manner considering how elegant the owner was and how far-reaching his empire. A man was standing at attention in front of him who wanted to be anywhere else but where he was at this particular moment.

"I want an answer," Silvio barked. "Why was my boat late in unloading, and why wasn't I informed of the delay?"

"There was a problem with one of the crew, and I had to take care of it on the spot," answered the man.

"What was this problem?"

"The usual—too much drink and too few brains. I straightened it out, but it took more time than I thought it would."

"The delay will cost me extra in wages that I have to pay to your crew."

The man became angry. "Look, you hired me to captain

the *Amanda Jane,* and you know I'm the best at what I do. The men trust me, and I trust them because I handpicked every one of them. Occasionally there's a minor error and I take care of it because damage control is necessary. I walk a tightrope for you, and there are times when you just have to cut me some slack. This was one of those times."

Silvio got up slowly from his chair, walked over to the man and placed a hand on his shoulder.

"Peter, Peter," he crooned softly, "I do trust you. You've worked for me for a long time, and you know that we hot-blooded Sicilians must blow off steam once in a while. I just prefer to know when things don't go according to plan, and I want to hear it personally."

"Then let me run my boat and do my job as I see fit. I made the decision not to worry you with a minor problem. Isn't it more important to get the catch unloaded than draw attention to a drunken crew member? If you feel strongly about the extra money you have to spend in overtime, then take it out of my end."

The two men stared at each other, and the undercurrent of the atmosphere was charged like the aftermath of an electric storm.

"I believe you did what you had to do," said Silvio, finally breaking the silence. "Can you continue to rely on your crew to keep their mouths shut?"

"Of course," replied the captain.

"Then we will say no more about it."

Silvio walked back to his desk and took an envelope from the top drawer. "I understand you have some happy news to report?"

"Yes, I'm getting married again, but how did you know?"

"I make it my business to know everything about my employees. Is she a local girl?"

"Yes, Diane is the librarian over in Bromfield and is widowed like me."

"Ah, but her late ex-husband was not a nice guy, was he?"

Peter inwardly winced at the words and wondered how this man knew about his plans and Diane's background.

"No, he wasn't, and she deserves everything good in the world, including a husband who will treat her well."

Silvio picked up the envelope and handed it to the captain.

"Buy your future bride something nice with my compliments," he said with a broad smile on his face.

But the smile did not reach his eyes, and the captain would recall that moment at a future date.

Chapter 15

Harry was now part of an FBI task force looking into the expanding drug problem on Boston's North Shore. Law enforcement was aware that the use of illegal drugs was becoming an epidemic, and the hospitals were now reporting overdoses regularly. It was clear that the root of the problem was the airtight distribution route, and following the trail from Colombia was going to be a key point if drug enforcement efforts were going to be successful. A sting operation was being reviewed, and the setup included several undercover agents acting as crew on fishing boats.

Going undercover was a part of his job that Harry disliked the most. It meant establishing street credibility, and his privileged lifestyle couldn't always conform to the role playing that was required. Today, the plan called for him to meet one of the major players, a fishing boat captain out of Gloucester. The man was approached months ago by the department, and he had finally agreed to become an informant.

Harry arranged by phone to meet him at a coffee shop a few miles from the waterfront. He wore jeans and a sweater, a knitted watch cap, worn sneakers, and borrowed an agency car.

It was late morning, and the heavy rain from the night before left muddy puddles on the pavement. The parking lot had plenty of empty spaces. Harry walked in and spotted the man wearing a plaid shirt under a puffy all-weather jacket sitting alone at the end of the counter reading a newspaper. He slid onto the empty stool next to him and ordered a cup of coffee and a donut. The morning crowd had thinned out, and they began to chat casually as two strangers might do.

"A good day to stay indoors," said Harry.

"If you can afford to be indoors," said the man, giving the correct prearranged answer.

Harry lowered his voice. "Thanks for agreeing to meet me. What have you got to report?"

The informant looked around casually and saw that he could speak freely.

"The Man is getting touchy lately, nervous that the catch isn't being unloaded fast enough. He called me on the carpet yesterday, but I was able to smooth things over. I think he's feeling the pinch from Colombia and he may be considering changing the route altogether."

"If he goes ahead with that, we'll have to ramp up surveillance."

"I'll be the first to know," observed the captain. "He'll want me to hire an additional crew, and I'll need time to do that. The stuff is hitting the street as fast as we can unload it."

They were silent again, sipping their coffees.

"Is there any chance he might make a move in the next few weeks?" Harry finally asked.

"That could be. I'm not due to take the *Amanda Jane* out again for a few days. I'll hang around the waterfront and keep my ears open."

"Thanks. Your efforts are very much appreciated," said Harry, leaving a bill and some change on the counter before he walked out the door.

He drove back to Boston to write up his report and was at his desk when Veronica called.

"Hi, my beloved," he crooned, answering the phone on the first ring.

"You always say the sweetest things," replied Veronica. "I'm calling to remind you about our dinner tonight at Poppies. Diane and her guy will meet us there at seven. I can't wait to meet him today when he comes in to pay for her engagement ring.

"She's so in love, Harry, and deserves to have a decent man in her life."

"I agree, and let's hope the happiness she feels now will always last."

Peter Parelli arrived at Veronica's Vintage at noon and introduced himself. Veronica observed that he didn't look at all like she had pictured him in her mind. Because of his occupation, she expected a tough, muscular man with shaggy hair, a beard, and rough hands. Instead, the fellow standing in front of her had short, neatly trimmed, slightly gray hair, no beard, and a tanned complexion. His large dark brown eyes had crinkled lines at the corners from years of squinting at the horizon. She greeted him warmly, and they walked over to her desk at the back of the store.

She took out a box and handed it to him. His face broke into a wide smile when he saw the ring.

"My lady sure has good taste," he said, examining the ring in the light. Veronica explained the finer points of the jewel, and when he heard the name of the famous New York store where it originally came from, he was very impressed.

"I have to say, Veronica, I would not have been able to afford this diamond if I had to purchase it from their store. I'm incredibly grateful to you for giving me this great price."

He pulled out his wallet and paid in cash. Veronica excused herself to gift wrap the package, and he took the opportunity to look in the jewelry cases.

"I see you carry men's items as well. I could use a new wristwatch, but I'm afraid these are much too fancy for a fisherman."

"If you like, I can keep an eye out for you. Give me an idea of what you're looking for because I never know what I'll find."

He laughed. "Oh, I need a heavy-duty model, one that's definitely waterproof."

Peter was thinking of the envelope of money that Silvio had given him and had made up his mind that he wouldn't spend any of it. He hated working for the man and knew it was only a matter of time before the FBI caught up with his boss, and he would be looking for work again.

He had wanted to be his own boss for years and had been putting away money to buy his boat. The insurance costs and maintenance fees for fishing boats had always been prohibitive. Fishing profits went up and down regularly, but he knew his skills as an experienced captain would always be in demand.

Before his wife died three years ago after being diagnosed with ovarian cancer, Peter thought about changing jobs. The cost of the drugs to treat her and the hospital bills almost bankrupted them. He had to refinance his house, and her insurance plan from work just barely covered the basics. Working at a desk job that only paid benefits wasn't for him. He decided to become the captain of his own boat, and that was his goal.

When the FBI approached him, the money they offered was one of the chief reasons he decided to go undercover. Peter had to be careful about how he handled their payments to him. He insisted on cash and opened an account under another name that couldn't be traced back to him. He couldn't take any chances that Silvio would ever find out about his involvement with law enforcement because he knew better than anyone the penalty would be a painful and horrible death.

After he proposed to Diane, they discussed the possibility of him giving serious thought to retirement. But the reality was he made good money, was still an age where he could reasonably work for at least another ten years, barring any physical problems, and he had the sea in his blood. If he ever took another job, it would have to be related to fishing because he couldn't picture himself in any other occupation. Good captains were always in demand, and Peter's reputation was golden.

Of course, Diane had no idea that her future husband was working as an informant for the FBI, and he did not plan on telling her anytime soon, if at all. Peter's beloved kid brother had died of a cocaine overdose five years before. The shock and horror of it had made him vow to do anything he could to avenge his death.

When the opportunity presented itself, and he was approached to report what he knew about drug trafficking on the docks, he decided to do anything he could to help take down Aldo Silvio and his dirty network. Even though the danger, if he was ever found out, was terrifyingly real, Peter knew he had to do it.

Silvio had his own way of dealing with snitches. Several months before, the body of another captain and one of his crew members was found hanging on grappling hooks, gutted like the fish they caught, their tongues cut out. The message was loud and clear: turn on me, and you will suffer the consequences.

Peter looked around Veronica's Vintage and commented on the pretty displays.

"I'm looking forward to meeting Harry tonight. Diane tells me he's in the art field and is a well-known collector. I regret that I know so little about paintings."

"Well, Peter, we know so little about your business, so we can all spend the evening learning some interesting things about one another."

Chapter 16

Violet Thompson arrived home after an exhausting day cleaning houses and bent over to pick up the mail on her front hall floor, all the while grumbling about her arthritis. She yelled out to Kevin to ask if he wanted a cup of coffee while struggling to get into the slippers that she kept by the coat rack in the hallway. The silence told her he was not home yet.

She walked into the kitchen, made coffee, and sat down with a stack of ten lottery tickets she had picked up at the convenience store on the way home, along with milk and bread. She carefully took the S&H Green Stamps from the bag and put them aside to paste into the coupon book. She almost had enough now to order a new toaster. She had asked Kevin repeatedly to fix her old one, but he never seemed to get around to it.

Violet adhered to this little ritual daily and it helped make her working life tolerable. Afterward, she would phone her sister, Marigold, who lived in Boston.

Their mother was fond of flowers and named each of her four girls after her favorite blossoms. The family joked about what name she would have come up with if she had spawned a son. Marigold had married an undertaker, a man who was guaranteed never to be out of work.

She reached for her lucky dime from the dish on the kitchen table and began to vigorously rub a dollar ticket from the pile of ten stacked in front of her.

"Nothing here," she said in disgust and shoved it aside. The second and third cards yielded no wins either. It wasn't until she scratched the eighth card that she suddenly sat up straight in her chair, pushed her eyeglasses back up her nose, and looked again.

"Yippee," she cried to the empty house. "Yippee, I won, I won."

She leaped from her chair and did a little dance around it three times, three being her lucky number. Violet's parents had emigrated from Ireland, and superstition was an important part of her upbringing. She reached for the card and peered at it again. Sure enough, the three pots of gold under the rainbow showed the same number 7 that the little leprechaun held in his hand.

Violet grabbed the phone and dialed Marigold's number.

"I'm a winner, sister," she screamed into the mouthpiece.

"What are you going on about, Violet?"

"I just scratched the winning Lotto Card."

"No kidding? How much did you get?"

"Five hundred bucks and on the 'Luck of the Irish' card too," she bragged.

"As it should be," said Marigold. "Now, don't go telling that son of yours, or he'll be hitting you up for some of it."

"A fine way for a godmother to talk," she admonished.

"Kevin is just going through a bad little patch, that's all. He'll be right as rain pretty soon. You'll see."

The conversation turned to how busy the funeral home was and who had died recently that they both knew. Violet walked out to the hall, put the winning ticket into her handbag, and went back into the kitchen to start dinner. She still had some pot roast left over from the night before, and she boiled some potatoes and carrots to round it out. Kevin walked into the house as she was shutting off the stove.

"Just in time to eat, son," she said. "Go and wash your hands before you sit down to dinner."

"Aw, stop treating me like a kid, Ma," he whined. "I don't need to wash my hands again."

"Okay," she said, kissing him on the forehead. "I still think of you as my little boy, so don't take that away from me," she said and set a brimming plate of hot food in front of him.

She sat and watched him devour his meal, smiled, and decided to take Marigold's advice for the time being and not say anything to him about her winning ticket. He sat back eventually and patted his belly. "No one can cook like my ma." Violet beamed at her son's compliment as though she had won the lottery twice.

"How are you coming along looking for another job?" she asked eventually. Kevin scowled and said he was helping a friend who owned a furniture moving company.

"Are you getting paid, or are you just doing him a favor?" she asked.

"He throws me a few bucks here and there."

She sighed and walked over to the sink to wash the

dishes. Kevin had disappeared into the hallway on his way upstairs and saw his mother's pocketbook on the table where she put the mail. He decided to help himself to some cash and reached in to retrieve her wallet when his hand brushed against the lottery ticket. He took it out and realized he was holding a windfall.

"So, she finally hit something," he said in wonder and tried to figure out how he could cash in on this stroke of luck.

He wondered if his mother was going to tell him about the win and tucked the ticket in his jeans pocket, deciding he needed the money more than she did. His poker winnings were slim lately, and he had heard about a game down on the waterfront he thought he might try. When she noticed it was missing and confronted him, he would deny he even knew about it and tell her she must have lost the ticket somewhere.

Kevin bounded up the stairs, happy in the knowledge that his newfound stash would keep him in the basics for a while, at least until he could collect what was owed him from his end of the drug sales. It seemed the money he made dealing drugs slipped through his fingers like water. He was losing more than winning at poker lately, and Mrs. Vee was taking her own sweet time paying him, and it didn't suit at all that he had to wait for his cut. Maybe it was time to go rogue and do a little dealing on his own. Yeah, he would look into that, and soon.

Chapter 17

Poppies Restaurant was located a little out of the town of Bromfield on a quiet road away from the waterfront. The building stood alone on a large lot and was converted from the original neat antique house, a large, two-story New England clapboard affair but with the addition of a wraparound veranda. When the Vickers first saw the property, they immediately envisioned their restaurant on this site. They added the veranda and the fancy fretwork designs along the railings and expanded the parking lot to include space for fifty vehicles.

Their idea was to offer gourmet fare for lunch and dinner to the discerning few who would become their valued repeat client base. Most evenings reservations gave them a full house, and on weekends, they always had a waiting list.

Tonight, the main dining room was softly lit with candles on each table. The entry hall featured an enormous bouquet of fresh flowers arranged in a large antique Chinese blue and white bowl. Diane and Peter arrived first, and when Veronica and Harry walked in, the men were surprised but showed no indication that they had met for the first time only the day before. They shook hands warmly as two strangers finding themselves in happy circumstances might do.

When their table was ready, the hostess led them to a quiet corner in front of a window that reflected the fairy lights hanging over an arbor that led to a rear garden. In good weather, this was a popular spot to sit in, but the wind was blowing what was left of the early autumn leaves around tonight, and the outdoor furniture had been put away for the season. The wine steward made his recommendations to Harry and the wine and champagne for toasting were ordered.

As the women complimented each other on their dresses, the men tried to act nonchalant. It wasn't often that Harry was surprised, but he had no idea that his undercover contact in the top-secret FBI drug sting operation he was working on was the fiancé of his girlfriend's best friend.

And here Peter was, sitting across from them at this celebration dinner. Of course, it was understood that the two men could not divulge their connection, and they both spent the rest of the evening attempting to maintain the charade of never having met each other.

"Diane and I want to thank you both for inviting us tonight," said Peter. "It really means a lot that you're happy for us." They all picked up their champagne flutes, clinked glasses, and toasted the engagement.

Diane kept staring at her hand, and Harry complimented her on how beautiful the ring was. The women giggled, and Veronica said she was delighted that Diane knew her own mind when it came to antique jewelry. The menus arrived, and the quartet became silent as they perused the offerings.

Eventually, Veronica said to Diane, "I never asked, but tell me how you two met."

"Can you believe we met at the library? One day, I was working at the checkout desk, relieving a colleague at lunchtime, when Peter walked in and asked where the historical maritime books were. Please don't laugh, but when I looked up and saw his face, I was smitten. There was something about him that I was instantly drawn to.

"I walked him over to the section that he wanted, and we chatted for a while. Pretty soon, I had to return to my own office at the back of the building. Recently, it dawned on me that if I hadn't been asked to relieve a coworker for lunch and spend an hour at the checkout desk, I might have never met this wonderful man."

"And that would have been a shame," said Peter, taking Diane's hand and kissing it, "because I would never have had the pleasure of this wonderful woman's love and company."

Diane continued. "He came in again on the pretext of looking for another type of book, woodworking, this time, I think, and asked for me. I was at a conference that day, and the woman who spoke with him said he became quite grumpy when he heard I wasn't there."

"I wasn't grumpy," Peter complained. "I just wanted to see you again. I'm afraid I bit off the poor woman's head, but she assured me that Diane would be back the next day. We were heading out to sea early in the morning, so I had to wait another week before I could return to the library."

Diane continued the tale. "When we met again, he brought me a box of chocolates and a container of caviar! I was surprised, to say the least, and couldn't, for the life of me, make the connection between the two gifts. He explained that the chocolates were because I was sweet to help him that day, and the caviar was the bounty of the sea."

"Nice touch," laughed Harry. "I don't suppose you had a bottle of champagne to go with the caviar?"

"I did have some in the car, but I didn't want to push my luck and overdo it. She agreed to go to dinner with me, and so, as they say, the rest is history."

The waiter arrived to take their orders. Veronica inquired if Benny Dalton was working as the chef that evening, and when he answered in the affirmative, she asked him to pass along her compliments.

The first course of baked Clams Casino arrived, which they all ordered. As they savored the delicious taste of the briny clams broiled with white wine, breadcrumbs, bacon, and green pepper, Peter asked Harry about his art collection.

"I understand, Harry, that you run a foundation that contains many world-famous artists' canvases. Did you acquire them yourself?"

Harry explained his family's history of collecting art, all the while knowing the person opposite him was wondering how he happened to be working for the FBI. So far, the two men still maintained the pretense of never having met before, each realizing the other was much more than he appeared to be.

The dinner progressed to the main course of baked stuffed lobster for Harry and Veronica and rack of lamb for Peter and Diane. When they had finished and were contemplating the dessert menu, Benny Dalton walked over to their table to say hello and graciously accepted their profuse compliments on their meals.

Veronica noted again Benny's brooding good looks and wondered, as all females do, if he had a woman in his life. She couldn't help but think that if Karen Little had her way, she would probably want to be that woman.

Then Patricia Vickers walked by the table to ask if their meals were satisfactory, and Veronica observed the look that Benny gave her, one of hopeful expectation and interest. It dawned on her that Benny was smitten with his employer and wondered if she returned his feelings.

The pianist played a repertoire of show tunes and could still be heard over the decibel level of the packed restaurant. Benny glanced again at Patricia, and they walked back toward the kitchen together.

"I wonder what's going on with those two," said Veronica. Diane turned her head and followed the retreating figures with her eyes.

"Do you think there's a love story there?" she asked.

Harry and Peter both laughed.

"Leave it to you women to cook up a romance!" said Harry.

"If that's a pun, Harry, I'll accept, but it's as plain as the nose on your face that Benny Dalton has feelings for Patricia Vickers."

"Her husband isn't even cold in his grave yet!" retorted Harry.

"That's a nasty turn of phrase, considering they found him in the restaurant's freezer."

They all laughed at Veronica's black humor despite themselves and returned their attention to the dessert menu.

Chapter 18

Kevin Thompson left the pool hall with a spring in his step. Not only had he just won a hundred-dollar bet by beating an old adversary, but he had also cashed in his mother's lottery ticket earlier in the evening. It had been a long time since he had been really flush, and he headed out to the poker game that he knew was going to be held in the basement of a bar on the waterfront. Luck was on his side tonight; he could feel it in his bones.

The guard at the door recognized him and let him enter. The room was already heavy with smoke, and he had to wait until a new game started. He was always a pretty good card player, but this game tended to be high stakes, and he was never sure he could risk playing here.

The money was now burning a hole in his pocket, and he confidently sat down and bought some chips. The beer he was drinking at the pool hall now turned into shots of whiskey, and he struggled to concentrate. His first three hands were washouts.

Then suddenly, things started to turn his way. Five pairs of eyes noticed the wad of cash he took out of his jeans pocket as he bought more chips. Two of the men around the table, in particular, watched him with interest. They knew a rube when they saw one, and as the evening progressed, Kevin became a marked man. His gambling luck held out, and he was almost five thousand dollars up when he decided to leave the game. Something told him it was time to cash in his chips.

He walked out of the basement room, unsteady on his feet, and stopped to light a cigarette in the alley before walking toward the waterfront to find a taxi. The night was chilly. He huddled into his pea jacket and tugged the top of his turtleneck sweater up to his ears. He sucked in some fresh air as he started to walk, only half-listening to the footsteps reverberating behind him in the darkened alley. He was thinking of the meeting he would have soon with Vee when she would pay him his cut for last week's drug sales.

Things were finally looking up. He had even been toying with the idea of buying a sports car, a bright red model, one that would be the envy of all those working stiffs on the production line at the plant. Yeah, he owed it to himself to buy something nice that would announce his new status. He'd been warned by Mrs. Vee to keep a low profile and to keep his mouth shut. Well, hadn't he been doing that? He wasn't stupid.

Suddenly, he sagged to the pavement in pain, and things started to go black. The two card sharks had knocked him on the side of his head with the handle of a gun, then moved quickly to divest him of his cash, but not before kicking him violently in the ribs a few times and dragging his limp body behind some trash cans.

It was awhile later before he came to, and he gingerly

reached up to feel the lump on his head while struggling to regain his footing. His left side hurt terribly, and the odor of rotting garbage from the trash cans caused him to upchuck before he was able to haul himself to a standing position and slowly walk away from the alley.

The tangy smell of the saltwater and cool air revived him a little as he tried to remember what had brought him to this place. When it finally dawned on him that he was a big winner playing poker, he shoved his hand into his jeans pocket for the roll of cash that he now remembered putting there.

All at once, it hit him through the throbbing pain in his head that the money was gone. Now he was out his winnings from the pool hall, the poker game, and his mother's lottery ticket. His ribs hurt, and blood was running down the side of his face. He could do nothing else but drag himself home.

———◉———

Violet realized she had to hurry. Tonight was her weekly bingo game at the American Legion Hall, and she had a feeling all day that she would be lucky. After all, didn't good luck always run in threes? First, she had her big lottery win, and winning tonight at bingo would enable her to buy more lottery tickets, and just maybe, they would turn out to be winners, as well.

Mrs. Vickers was due to pay her tomorrow, but she had just enough money in her wallet to pay for tonight's cards. She had decided to wait before she cashed in her ticket and went into her handbag to retrieve it so that she could hide it in her bedroom in the little tin candy box she kept under the bed.

She rummaged around in her bag but couldn't seem to put her hands on it. Exasperated, she grabbed the pocketbook and dumped the contents onto the kitchen table, sifting through an assortment of used paper tissues, keys, various prescription bottles, cough drops, and her wallet.

"It has to be here," she mumbled in frustration, "I know it's here because I remember putting it in just before I started dinner."

Suddenly, the penny dropped. Kevin took it. He must have opened her bag and helped himself to the ticket before he left the house tonight. Violet sank onto the nearest chair and started to cry.

"How could he do that to me?" she wailed. "He knows I need the money to run the house, and I was looking forward to putting a little by to start a nest egg for myself." She was beside herself with sadness and frustration.

After a while, she stood up, took off her apron, and put her hat and coat on. A night at bingo was just what she needed. Spending time with the friends she had made there would take her out of herself. She knew she had to get away from the house tonight, and the knowledge that her son was just plain selfish and cruel wasn't going to put a damper on her evening. She would confront Kevin later.

Chapter 19

The patrol car pulled up in front of the small apartment building on a quiet side street, and the officer walked into the lobby and pressed the bell for Dalton-2B. It took awhile for Benny to answer, and when he opened the door, he immediately recognized Lt. Phil Balducci.

"Did I wake you, Mr. Dalton?" he asked.

"I worked late last night at the restaurant, Lieutenant, and am due back this afternoon." He invited him to sit down and asked if he wanted a cup of coffee.

"No thank you, sir, but I do have a few questions for you."

"Sure, but let me make a cup for myself, or else I won't make any sense to you." He padded over to the kitchen in his bare feet and pulled out the coffeepot, the belt of his bathrobe trailing on the floor.

Balducci looked around the small but neat living room lined with shelves and lots of books. The furniture was sparse, but the quality was good. There were no family pictures or mementos, and the feeling he got was of a man who valued his privacy.

Dalton came back with his mug and sat down opposite

Balducci. "What brings you here this morning, Lieutenant?"

"I've become aware that you didn't disclose some valuable information to us when we interviewed you after your attack. I just need you to fill in the blanks for me now, sir."

Benny took a sip, put the mug down, and scratched his chin. "Well, I suppose you mean that I had once worked for Robert Vickers and then quit?"

"Yes. Can you tell me why you left?"

"Because the man was a selfish, boorish, pompous Philistine, that's why!"

"Is this a work-related opinion, or did the two of you just not get along for personal reasons?" asked Balducci, taking out a small notebook and jotting down notes.

"Both. He treated me and the staff like we were low-life forms, not worthy of working with the great restaurant owner that he aspired to be."

"I was under the impression, sir, that Mr. Vickers was a successful restaurant owner."

"Thanks to talented and creative chefs like me and his wife who ran things in the background and generally propped him up. He went through staff like water because no one could stand to be in the same kitchen with him once they got a bellyful of his ego and bad attitude."

"So, are you telling me you quit, or were you fired?"

Benny took another sip of his coffee. "I quit before I was fired."

"I see. Do you think the attack on you had anything to do with your decision to leave Poppies?"

Benny hesitated for a moment before answering. "You know, Lieutenant, I've given that question a great deal of thought, and I wouldn't be at all surprised if the jerk arranged it."

"For what reason, do you think? Retaliation?"

"I can certainly see him doing a dirty, underhanded thing like that. Right up his alley."

"And yet, Mr. Vickers was killed in his restaurant right after you left his employ."

"I had an airtight alibi, Lieutenant, as you well know. I was working at The Helping Hand that night at the alleged time of his death, as dozens of witnesses can attest. I never left my post."

"Yes, sir, that is true. But, of course, a third party could have murdered him."

Benny jumped up from the couch, his fists clenched at his side. "Are you saying I took out a contract to have him killed?"

"Easy, sir, easy. Sit down, please. You have quite a temper there. I'm suggesting that any animosity you had with Robert Vickers could have prompted his death. But, as you say, many other people disliked him as well."

Benny sat down again and ran his fingers through his hair. "I'm sorry, but Vickers is still a sore spot with me. I'm also sorry he died a violent death, but I didn't do it or arrange for it. Yes, I hated him, but not enough to murder him."

"Did he get along with Mrs. Vickers at work?"

"Oh, he bossed Patricia around too, but don't worry, she knew enough to stay out of his way when he was in one of his foul moods. It was because of her that some of us stayed. Several people had told me that when they first opened the business together, he couldn't have been nicer ... the complete opposite of what he had become. I don't know what happened to make him the way he was when I worked there. I can only comment on my experience with him."

"What was your experience with Mrs. Vickers?"

"I always got along well with Patricia. If it weren't for her, I'd have left long ago. After he was murdered, Patricia asked me to come back as head chef, and I accepted. The terms of my employment are excellent, and the salary is great, but most of all, I'm my own man. I'm the head chef in every way."

He waved his arm around the room. "As you can see, Lieutenant, I live simply. I don't need expensive trinkets or knickknacks to be happy. I'm a creative person, and I express that creativity in the kitchen. I just want to be left alone to do my job."

Balducci closed his notebook, put it into his jacket pocket, and stood up. "Thank you for your time, Mr. Dalton. I may have more questions for you later on, so don't plan on leaving Bromfield any time soon."

Benny nodded his assent and walked him to the door. Balducci left with questions that still had not been answered.

Chapter 20

The black Cadillac limousine arrived at Poppies, this time parking at the rear of the building, and the driver and the bodyguard both remained in the car. Patricia opened the back door of the kitchen, and she and Silvio immediately went into the office. The restaurant was empty . . . No one around to hear the sounds of their lovemaking. She looked forward to his visits, and they were becoming more frequent.

Aldo was an important man, and that made him irresistible to her. Even though she could only guess at the extent of his drug kingdom, he was educated and sophisticated and knew how to treat a woman. Patricia remembered how Robert used to be when they were first married. They had so much in common, and their love and commitment to each other helped propel them to success. But that was long ago, and the here and now for her was Aldo Silvio, who was still a potent lover even at his age.

Now that Robert was no longer in the equation, she was quite happy to let Aldo run things while he left her to her baking and the day-to-day running of the successful restaurant. He was the perfect silent partner, and they had even recently discussed the possibility of opening another restaurant, this time a seafood grille at a location farther up the coast. He saw to it that there were funds to pay the bills on time, and the team she hired, especially Benny Dalton, worked well together. There were very few problems now, and Patricia knew Aldo would take care of anything else. She only had to ask.

Of course, Patricia knew that the cover of a successful restaurant suited Aldo Silvio's drug operation, and she happily left that side of the business to him. Her only involvement concerned the actual shipment drop-offs to Poppies. She was also in charge of accepting and checking the packets and paying the two and sometimes three dealers their share. Beyond that, she had no interest or desire to be involved with the drug business.

The plan was that she would pay off the two men who had unloaded the last shipment from the plane. But word had reached Aldo that one of the men, Kevin Thompson, had been drunk and was robbed on the waterfront the night before. He was heard bragging that he was involved with a "big money operation" and was becoming a liability and had to be eliminated. There could be no loose ends.

Patricia had always questioned who actually killed Robert. She assumed it was Aldo who ordered the murder, and he as much as admitted it to her. Robert had become a problem to their partnership, getting out of control with his mounting gambling debts and black moods, and Aldo could no longer trust him to hold up his end of their agreement.

It had always bothered Patricia that she was never made aware of the terms of their deal. She only knew that Poppies was in jeopardy because the bills were not being paid. Robert had shut her out of the business end of the restaurant entirely.

Then again, it could be said that Benny Dalton, whom Patricia was quite confident had romantic feelings for her, may have arranged for the murder. She was aware that he had a hair-trigger temper, and his hatred of Robert for his treatment of her at work was evident to her and anyone else who worked with them. She also saw a side of Benny, a soft side that few people knew about, but that still didn't leave him out as a suspect either.

Robert had huge gambling debts with some serious people, and the loan shark he was involved with was not to be trifled with. Perhaps Robert just hadn't made payments on time, and this man would be happy to use him as an example to others who had ideas of not repaying on a timely basis. Patricia still wasn't quite prepared to accept that Aldo actually had her husband killed.

So, that's three people as chief suspects for murdering Robert, and she ticked them off on her fingers. She was sure she could come up with more names if she put her mind to it.

Benny was due to come in to prepare for the lunch business. Even though he had worked late the night before, he promised to take this shift after the other sous chef asked to switch for personal reasons. She sighed. This was always a problem in the restaurant business. Thankfully, Benny was always there when she needed him.

If she was honest, she realized that she was thinking about Benny more and more lately. He was very handsome, a true talent in the kitchen, and she had no doubt he was talented in the bedroom as well. She was also aware that his brooding nature and beautiful eyes turned female heads regularly. He was intelligent too but kept himself to himself. Yes, Benny Dalton was a man she could let her hair down with, in more ways than one.

Patricia was in the kitchen kneading dough for the bread that she had made the restaurant famous for. The back-and-forth motion and the tactile feel of the dough always gave her a happy, satisfied feeling. She knew the end product would be delicious, and the smell of baking bread filled the place when Benny walked in.

"Hi, Benny, It's good of you to help with Charlie's shift this afternoon. I really appreciate it."

"No problem, Patricia. To be honest, I'm happy for the distraction. I had a visit this morning from a police lieutenant regarding Robert's case."

She stopped kneading abruptly and looked up. "What did he want?"

"He just wanted to go over some of the facts about the attack on me as well as events at the restaurant before Robert was killed."

Patricia winced at the word, and Benny noticed it immediately. "I'm sorry to bring it all up again, but you did ask the question."

"No, no, it's all right, Benny. Believe me. What's done is done, and I'm coming to grips with it."

Benny hung up his coat in the closet and came over and patted her softly on her shoulder. She turned into him, and they put their arms around each other and hugged. She started to cry, and he could feel her hot tears on his neck.

"It's okay; get it out of your system," he said softly. He

took her chin in his hand and wiped away some tears with the other. They looked into each other's eyes and suddenly it went from a tender moment to a passionate one, and he kissed her hard on the lips. She responded with fervor.

The slam of the back door by one of the prep chefs carrying a large carton of onions into the kitchen was like a cannon shot. Patricia and Benny quickly broke apart and darted in different directions.

The spell was broken. They went about their duties for the rest of the day as if nothing had happened. It was almost as if the tender interlude was a regular occurrence and, in truth, it was, but only in their minds and imaginations.

Chapter 21

It was turning out to be a busy morning at Veronica's Vintage. A sale was advertised for the weekend, and it wasn't often the shop had one. Veronica had to clean out some stock to make room for newer items recently purchased. Teens from Bromfield High were starting to shop regularly, and they were particularly interested in the vintage leather boots and high-heeled shoes. The college crowd also wanted the vintage boots, and their taste ran to funky jewelry as well. Their mothers gravitated toward the sweaters and suits, and both purchased from the large selection of vintage handbags and jewelry.

Due to the popularity of the television series, *Dynasty*, older customers wanted flashy rhinestone costume jewelry and embellished clothing with sequins and pearls that radiated glamour and sophistication to go with their teased hairdos. Padded shoulders and nipped-in waistlines, fashionable in the late war years, were once again the favored silhouette, and lovers of vintage clothing scoured the racks for pieces with that look, especially in the color pink.

Susan, Veronica's helper, had become adept at wrapping

packages quickly and today she was busy at the cash register as well as the credit card machine. The morning seemed to fly and the early afternoon store traffic was still still strong with shoppers coming in during their lunch hour. Diane arrived with two salads and they went to the back room to eat.

"I really need a Cobb salad today, but mostly, I just need to sit down and rest my feet," said Veronica. She took off her harlequin glasses and laid them on the table. "What's new with you and Peter?"

"After that wonderful dinner at Poppies the other night, we went back to my apartment and talked some more about the future. Peter was seriously thinking about retirement a few months ago but for some reason that plan doesn't seem to be as important to him as it once was.

"I just want him to be happy, Ronnie, but I don't mind telling you I worry like mad when he's at sea. When he came home after this last trip, I noticed a change in his personality."

"What do you mean?"

"Well, I can't really put it in words, but he seemed more introspective, more serious. I asked him if he had any problems with the crew, but all he would tell me was that some things were changing that he had no control over. When I asked for details, he refused to answer."

"I know what you're saying. Sometimes, when I ask Harry details about his work, he changes the subject. I feel a little left out, but I know too that we agreed long ago to give each other space, and I have to respect that."

Diane put her fork down. "Do you think I should do the same with Peter, or am I going into a marriage where there will be secrets? I couldn't take that again because Carl kept secrets that eventually led to his death. Remember what a mess I was when you first met me?"

"I don't think Peter could ever be compared with Carl, but only you can know that."

"Thank God they are nothing alike, Ronnie. Peter is a wonderful man, but deep down, I still worry that I'll repeat some of the same mistakes that I've made in the past by believing everything I hear. I want this relationship to last and know I could never endure any more lies and deceit."

Veronica understood the anxiety that Diane was experiencing and realized that her friend was feeling compromised. Sometimes she felt the same with Harry but in her case, she knew his background as an undercover agent prevented her from knowing important details about his working life.

"I think you're marrying a complex man, but maybe you just have to give him some scope and trust that what he does or will do will always keep you safe and secure. You love him for all the right reasons, but I've learned from my own experience that the life your man had before he met and fell in love with you will always color his actions."

There was a knock on the door, and Susan put her head in. "I'm sorry to interrupt your lunch, Ronnie, but a customer has a question about a piece of jewelry she wants to buy."

"Thanks, Susan. Tell her I'll be right there." She turned to Diane. "Stay here and finish your lunch. Don't worry about Peter. He will come around and let you know when the time comes."

Diane sighed again. "I hope you're right."

Chapter 22

Violet woke up the next morning in a much better mood. Her lucky night at the bingo game almost made up for the disappointment of Kevin stealing her lottery ticket. She won a game all by herself that paid fifty dollars, then won again when she split a game with another player for twenty-five dollars. And, wonder of wonders, they pulled her ticket for the door prize of twenty dollars. Her belief that luck always came in threes had again come true, and now she had to deal with her son.

Before she started breakfast, she made sure that her cleaning supplies for the day were ready to go. Today, she had Patricia Vickers, then Ada Perkins to work for. She put the bacon on to fry and called up to Kevin to come down to breakfast. When he didn't appear, she yelled up the stairs again.

"Come down and eat, Kevin. I have to leave for work pretty soon." When he didn't respond, she walked upstairs to wake him. His back was turned when she opened the bedroom door, and as she walked over to shake him, she noticed a bloody tee shirt on the floor.

"Kevin, get up. I have to talk to you," she demanded. He rolled over, and her heart almost stopped as she barely recognized her own son. His face was black and blue and swollen, and his hair was matted with dried blood. He moaned, and she rushed over and struggled to help him into a sitting position.

"What's happened?" she cried. "What trouble did you get yourself in?"

"I hurt, Ma, so don't yell at me."

"Who beat you up, Kevin Thompson, and where is my lottery ticket?"

"I need coffee and some aspirin. Can you get me some?"

"Answer me, Kevin. What's going on?"

"I'll talk after I get cleaned up," he said, struggling to get out of bed. Violet saw him clutch his ribs and stagger into the bathroom.

Eventually, he came into the kitchen and gingerly sat down at the table. She placed a plate of bacon, eggs, and toast in front of him next to a mug of steaming coffee and sat down across from him while he struggled to eat. Her eyes never left his face while she silently acknowledged to herself that she would never see any of the money she had won.

"Well, I'm waiting for an explanation, son."

Kevin kept his eyes on the plate in front of him and mumbled, "I ran into a couple of guys at a card game, and they beat me up and robbed me."

"Did you take my lottery ticket, Kevin?"

"I was goin' to cash it in for you, Ma, and give you the money and my winnings from the card game, but they must have known I had a roll in my pocket."

"Don't lie to me, Kevin Thompson. I've had enough of your lies!"

"I told you not to yell, Ma. My head hurts. Everything hurts."

Violet glanced at the clock on the wall. "I have to go to work now but when I get home we'll talk about this some more, and I want answers. But mostly, I want the money back that you took from me."

"Don't worry. I'll have some money for you tonight," he mumbled.

She stood up, put on her coat and hat, and walked out the door banging the screen door behind her, leaving him with his head bowed over the plate. Eventually, he got up and showered, then went back to bed for another couple of hours, his body still sore from his injuries. He knew he would be getting paid at the restaurant tonight for his cut from the last shipment of cocaine. He would pay back some of the money he owed to his mother and hoped that would keep her quiet for a while.

Chapter 23

Benny arrived early at Poppies and immediately started to prepare for the afternoon lunch service. The fresh vegetables and meat he had ordered had arrived, and some helpers were busy unloading the boxes. Patricia came out of her office to supervise the fruit and dairy deliveries. The two chefs smiled at each other as they worked in tandem. Everyone in the kitchen worked well together. There was no drama or dominant personalities . . . just professionals doing a job they all loved.

Patricia looked over at one point and stared at Benny's profile. He looked up abruptly and saw her staring at him and realized that he wanted to kiss her very badly.

The phone rang in her office. She rushed to answer it, closing the door behind her.

"Hello, my dear. Are you having a good morning?" inquired Aldo Silvio.

"All the better at hearing your voice," she cooed.

"I'm calling to let you know that you will be receiving a cash delivery today to pay the dealers this evening. However, there will be a personnel change, and this will be

Kevin Thompson's last job."

"May I ask why?"

"Let's just say he is no longer able to operate in a trust-worthy manner and leave it at that."

"All right, Aldo, whatever you say. I don't want to know the details, and I'll act as if I don't know."

"Perfect, as always, my dear. I will see you soon." And the phone call ended.

She wondered what Kevin had been up to, to prompt his decision. Patricia hung up the phone and walked back out to the kitchen. Benny was in the storeroom sorting out vegetables, and she went and stood beside him and reached for his hand. He turned and smiled and glanced around to see if anyone was in sight before he kissed her.

"I've been waiting to do that for quite some time," he whispered.

"So have I," she said and returned his kiss.

"I know, Patricia, that it's probably not a good idea to do this here."

"You're right, and we can fix that soon."

"Tonight? At my apartment?" he asked.

"I'll be working here late on the books but maybe to-morrow," she said, knowing that if Aldo found out she was romancing her chef that he wouldn't be at all pleased.

They heard footsteps close by and broke apart quickly. This is turning out to be an interesting day for me, thought Patricia.

Chapter 24

The day was turning out to be busy for Harry as well, especially now that high-level agents from the Special Task Force for Drugs were flying in from New York and Washington for a meeting called to examine findings from recent intelligence gathered through the Boston office of the FBI.

The authorities had determined that the drug cartels originating in Colombia had been stepping up production, and their distribution line to Canada and down to the East Coast was flourishing. An alarming increase in cocaine over-doses had recently been reported by law enforcement resulting from the cutting of the raw material with harmful agents such as heroin to make a potentially lethal cocktail known as a speedball.

Other additives were used like caffeine, boric acid, laxatives, and even laundry detergent to cut the pure cocaine and stretch profits for the dealers. Users didn't know or care that they weren't buying a pure product, and the ingestion of these substances was hazardous to the brain and organs through constant use.

The trail of distribution to the New England area started with private planes making drug drops to Silvio's fleet of fishing boats. The drug enforcement agencies knew it was virtually impossible to police the entire North Atlantic. There would never be enough equipment and personnel, and the drug dealers knew this. Only intelligence gathered through undercover means could pinpoint the operation.

Harry made his report to the group from details gathered from his talk with the man he now knew as Peter Parelli, a pivotal informant in the FBI's plan. He arranged to meet Peter in the parking lot of a busy Bromfield supermarket after their dinner at Poppies.

"Thanks for agreeing to see me again, Peter. I know the chance you're taking here."

"Silvio wants me to go back out to sea in two days to take in another drop. The product is in high demand, and he needs to offload it so that it reaches the street as soon as possible."

"Okay, but this time, both the DEA and the Coast Guard will be monitoring your boat and the plane that will make the drop. Thanks for the coordinates, by the way. They will help us a lot."

"I just want to nail this bastard, Harry, for me and for the brother I lost and for the families and loved ones of those who are still hooked on the junk."

"As long as Silvio is still in the dark about your involvement with us," cautioned Harry.

"Don't worry. I have no wish to become collateral damage to Aldo Silvio's drug empire. As far as he knows, I'm a fishing boat captain who follows his instructions to the letter."

"The Bureau can't afford to lose an important link like you, and we will cover your back, always. And I can't afford to lose my girl's best friend's future husband, or they would both kill me. We need to get Silvio, Peter. We have to take him down as soon as possible."

"And I have to get my life together for my new bride."

Unfortunately, he had no way of warning Diane what was coming. He prayed there would be no publicity if he were ever arrested for his role, and protecting his true identity would keep him alive. He couldn't reveal any of this to her, and he hoped that when she finally learned the truth about his job, she could forgive him for not being honest with her. She would have to understand that he was protecting her as well as himself. Silvio would not hesitate to go after his future wife either.

Diane had made it clear that trust was the most important thing to her at the very start of their relationship. She said she couldn't go forward with their marriage if they were going to keep secrets from each other. Her marriage to Carl was a sham, she told him, because he always lied to her. She never knew if he was telling her the truth about his activities or anything about his job and didn't want to ever go through that again.

Peter struggled with this conflict, and now, just before their marriage, the biggest test of their love for each other was going to happen, and in the possible glare of publicity. But even more importantly, his life was going to be in danger if Aldo Silvio found out he was a mole. The penalty in the Mafia for betrayal is death—his and probably Diane's as well. How could he tell her that because she loved him, she could die?

Chapter 25

"I'm finally going to get paid," said Kevin to himself, as he drove to Poppies at 1:15 a.m. He pulled into the darkened parking lot and entered the restaurant by the unlocked kitchen door. He walked into the office where Patricia was talking to two other dealers. A box of cash lay opened in front of her on the desk where she sat, unsmiling, tapping her fingernails on the top.

"You're late," she barked, looking pointedly at her watch.

"Sorry, Mrs. Vee, but I had to be sure I wasn't being followed driving over here."

She wasn't surprised to see his black and blue swollen face because Aldo had already told her about his injuries, but she asked anyway.

"Do you want to tell me where you got that face?"

"I was rolled after a poker game at the waterfront by a couple of card sharks. I never saw them coming."

"So you were drunk too?" she asked.

"Yeah, I had a couple. What's it to you?"

"Look, Kevin," said Patricia through clenched teeth, "remember you are only here because I say you can be, so keep your sarcasm to yourself. I can't take any chances that you'll shoot your mouth off to the wrong people about my operation when you're so drunk that you can be robbed and kicked around."

Kevin was immediately able to see his predicament, and he followed Patricia out to the other part of the kitchen.

"Look, I'm sorry, Mrs. Vee. It won't happen again. I was just in the wrong place at the wrong time—that's all. It was a one-time thing. You know I keep my mouth shut."

His eyes started to water, and he sneezed a couple of times. He was standing in front of a colander of lobster and crab shells that would be boiled down to make stock for chowder.

Patricia stared at him wordlessly until he dropped his eyes to his folded hands. She handed him a stack of bills without further comment, and the other two dealers standing there quickly pocketed their money as well.

"That's all," she snapped. "You can all go. "I'll let you know when the next shipment is due to arrive."

They left, feeling a decided chill in the air from her argument with Kevin. After the door closed, Patricia went back to the office, picked up the telephone, and dialed Aldo Silvio, the lateness of the hour of no consequence.

Violet stayed awake as long as she could after coming home from bingo. On the one hand, she was elated by the night's wins and almost phoned Marigold to tell her about her good luck. She quickly decided against it, realizing sooner or later, she would be asked by her sister how she would spend her lottery win. She could never keep a secret from Marigold and couldn't face the recriminations about how much of a black sheep Kevin was.

Violet sighed and put on another pot of coffee. Kevin should be home by now, but lately, he had been staying out late. She wanted to know who these "friends" were and the true story about his injuries. She really should have insisted he go directly to the hospital emergency room but knew he would never do it. There was nothing to watch on television at this hour, and trying to concentrate on reading a book was out of the question, so she gave up waiting and walked upstairs to bed.

It was after 2:30 a.m. when Kevin finally arrived home. His mood was elevated because he had a wad of cash in his pocket again. Not feeling the least bit guilty, he counted out two hundred and fifty dollars and put it on the dining room table, anchoring the bills under the bowl of waxed fruit his mother always kept there. He realized it was only half of what she would have gotten if she had cashed in her lottery ticket, but he told himself there was no point in giving it to her all at once. She would only spend it.

He had stopped at a liquor store earlier before he went to Poppies, took the whisky bottle out of the paper bag, and poured himself a shot. It still hurt to move his arm, and he had to drink out of the corner of his mouth that wasn't swollen.

He sat on the couch with his drink and mentally vowed he wouldn't go back to that card game again alone. He should have left when he was ahead, but those two guys had probably earmarked him right away. He realized that he was stupid to show the roll in his pocket all at once. Next time, he would just have to watch it and refilled his glass until the bottle was half-empty. Soon his eyes closed, and he fell asleep, snoring fitfully.

The plaintive cry of a little white hoot owl pierced the quiet of the night as a window at the dining room side of the house was silently pulled up, the screen cut through with a sharp blade. The intruder slipped into the house without any trouble. He followed the noise of the sleeping figure on the couch and shined his flashlight on the plastic bag he was carrying. He reached his gloved hand in and pulled out a fistful of freshly shelled shrimp and while standing over the man, pried open his mouth and shoved the shrimp into it.

It took a few seconds for the realization of what was happening to him to register in his brain. Kevin's eyes snapped open, and he tried to spit out what was now choking him. The man bent over and clamped both hands around the victim's mouth while shoving his head against the cushion. Kevin tried to grab at the man's leather jacket but couldn't get hold of it. His breathing became labored . . . and soon stopped altogether.

When the man was satisfied that his quarry was dead, he quickly departed from the house the same way he had come in.

Chapter 26

The noisy cries of the owl outside her window woke Violet from her sleep. She glanced over at the clock on the bedside table. It read 4:40 a.m. She sighed heavily, turned on the light, got into her slippers, and walked down the hall to Kevin's room. She saw that his bed was still not slept in and started to worry. The only thing to do was make a pot of coffee and be ready to have it out with him when he walked in the front door. She went downstairs to the kitchen.

Violet had never liked confrontation of any kind. In fact, when her husband, Gerald, was alive, she would often just bite her tongue instead of arguing with him. It simply wasn't in her nature to scream and yell but, by God, if Kevin couldn't give her an explanation about why he stole the ticket out of her pocketbook, she would know the reason why. Her Irish dander was up, and enough was enough.

She carried her coffee mug into the living room to see if there was anything to watch on television, then stopped in her tracks when she saw Kevin, slumped on the couch, his mouth full of something pink. It took her a moment to register that he had eaten shrimp, and she knew very well that shrimp was deadly to him.

She ran over and tried to shake him, but his color was gray, and he wasn't breathing. Violet grabbed a fistful of her hair and pulled at it, then let out a lingering, high-pitched scream as the horror of the situation sank in. Quickly, she ran over to the telephone and dialed 911.

When the ambulance and police arrived, the news they gave her was what she already knew. Kevin had died from suffocation brought on by anaphylactic shock, an allergic reaction caused by his shellfish allergy that swelled his throat and cut off his breathing.

The question was, where did the shrimp that was crammed down his windpipe come from? A kindly policeman asked if someone could come over to stay with her, but Violet shook her head, and the medical attendant gave her a mild sedative. She closed her eyes as she sat on a chair , still in a state of shock.

About half an hour later, Lieutenant Phil Balducci and a policewoman entered the house. Violet was awake and drowsy but was able to answer their questions.

"I am very sorry for your loss, Mrs. Thompson," Lieutenant Balducci said. "I understand that it was you who discovered the body of your son?"

"Yes, it was me. I was waiting for him to come home so I could talk to him about an important family matter. As I told the sergeant earlier, Kevin's bed had not been slept in, so I came down to the kitchen to make some coffee and wait for him here in the living room. That's when I found him." She started to cry, and the policewoman handed her the box of tissues from a side table.

"Take your time, Mrs. Thompson," he said. "I know this is hard for you, but in cases of a suspicious death, we have to ask a lot of detailed questions."

Violet nodded and patted her wet eyes with the tissue. "I'll be all right now, Lieutenant."

"It appears that your son's mouth was crammed with cooked shrimp. Can you think of a reason why that would happen?"

"It doesn't make any sense. Kevin had an allergy to all shellfish and would never eat it. I couldn't even bring lobster, crab, shrimp, oysters, or clams into the house because he would break out in a rash and get sick immediately just being around it."

Balducci scribbled in his notebook. "So, is there any way he would have voluntarily eaten a meal of shrimp?"

"Not in a million years. He knew he would get deathly ill." She started to cry again.

"Can you explain why he has cuts and bruises all over his body?"

"He came home like that yesterday and wouldn't tell me how it happened."

A crime scene officer walked up to Balducci and whispered in his ear.

He turned to Violet. "My officer tells me that the side window over there was jammed up to the top, and the screen was cut out. We think that's how your son's assailant entered the house."

Violet walked over and examined the window. "No, the screen was never cut before. It's the first time I've seen it like this."

"We'll try to extract fingerprints if we can, but it appears the intruder was wearing gloves."

The policewoman tapped Balducci on the shoulder, and he followed her over to the dining room table. When he returned, he asked Violet why two hundred and fifty dollars in cash was under a bowl of waxed fruit on the table. She looked up in surprise and ran over to see for herself.

"I didn't notice that before," said Violet, and recounted the story of how Kevin stole the winning lottery ticket from her pocketbook, and that was the reason why she was waiting up for him to come home . . . to have it out with him.

"We are aware that Kevin has a police record, Mrs. Thompson. Mostly petty things when he was young, but more recently, serious charges were about to be brought against him. Did you know that?"

Violet's eyes were like saucers. "What kind of charges?"

Balducci watched her carefully. "He was dealing drugs here in Bromfield, mostly cocaine and heroin."

She was quiet for a long moment, a look of confusion on her face. "Was that why someone beat him up?" she finally asked.

"Could be," he answered. "Did you know that Kevin was dealing drugs, Mrs. Thompson?"

"Oh, that can't be right. My Kevin was a lot of things, but a drug dealer? No, I swear on my mother's memory, I had no idea what he was up to. All I know is that he always needed money but never took the trouble to look for a steady job. I was after him day after day to find anything else to do that would get him out of that pool hall."

"Then can you explain where this money came from?"

said Balducci, nodding his head toward the table.

"He told me yesterday he would have my money for me when I got home. He probably cashed in the lottery ticket that was worth five hundred dollars. I don't know why he didn't give me the whole amount."

"Did anyone in the family or any of his friends know about his allergy to shellfish?"

"Oh, I'm sure most of the family knew about it. We've known he was allergic since he was a young boy. He ate some oysters once and got deathly ill and had to be rushed to the hospital emergency room. I don't know that he ever mentioned it to any of his friends."

Violet started to cry again and asked the policewoman to call her sister Marigold to ask if she would come over and stay with her.

It was clear now to Balducci that Kevin Thompson was murdered. He was as much a victim as anyone else who was killed with a deadly weapon, with the same results that a fatal gun or knife wound could inflict.

He took a licorice stick from his jacket pocket, unwrapped the cellophane covering, and chewed thoughtfully. *This is a new one even for me,* he thought: *death by shrimp.*

Chapter 27

Diane discussed her idea of a wedding luncheon with Veronica. She planned on being married by a justice of the peace late in the morning, then on to the celebration directly following the ceremony at a local restaurant. Since both she and Peter had small families, and most of their friends lived locally, Diane thought they should limit their choices to the Greater Bromfield area.

"Why not call Patricia at Poppies, Diane? You enjoyed your meal there, and I'm sure she could accommodate your small wedding party in one of their function rooms."

"I was thinking along the lines of a more casual place, but Peter said he would leave the decision up to me. He just wants to be married soon, before the Thanksgiving and Christmas holidays. It doesn't leave much time for me to pull something together...just a couple of weeks really. Wait a minute ... I've got an idea. Why don't you come with me and help me make up my mind?"

"Are you sure you want my help, Diane?"

"Veronica Howard, you are officially and unofficially my best friend. Of course, I want your help. You've got impeccable taste, and you know me as well as anyone ... even better than Peter. Oh, say you will!"

"I'd be honored, really," said Veronica, a tear forming in her eye that she was trying to keep from running down her face.

"No, I'm the one who is honored that you will be at my side on the big day. Peter and I are so pleased you and Harry will be standing as witnesses for us, Ronnie. I can't tell you how much it means to me that you will be there to share my special day with my special man."

"We are delighted you asked us. Honestly, I can't think of anyone I know who better deserves to have happiness in marriage. I remember when we first met, and you were so miserable with Carl, trying to get past all the disappointment that you had with him. He was never who he seemed to be, but now, it's as if the stars have been realigned for you. I will plan your bridal shower, and you'll soon officially be Mrs. Peter Parelli."

"You're the only one who realizes that the right man has finally come into my life, someone who loves me totally who has no dark secrets, no hidden agendas, and no ties to crime. I have to pinch myself sometimes to believe my good luck that I've finally found a man who is everything I've always wanted in a husband."

The two women hugged, comrades and friends, sharing a moment of a happy expectation.

Diane took Veronica's suggestion and called Patricia Vickers for an appointment. She invited the two women to come by the restaurant the next morning to discuss menu suggestions for the wedding luncheon. Poppies Restaurant was a popular venue for receptions. They were encouraged to learn that the small function room would be available in three weeks due to a recent last-minute cancellation. They chose a menu based on twenty people, and Diane was still surprised that the cost was so high for so few guests. After consulting the function menu and considering the various suggestions from Patricia, Diane made her choices.

The meal would start with a classic clear consommé soup, followed by cannelloni pasta stuffed with ground pork, Romano cheese, spinach, and mushrooms. It would be served in a light tomato sauce, a nod to Peter's Italian heritage. The main course would consist of pan-seared medallions of veal accompanied by risotto and steamed broccoli in a lemon sauce. Patricia's famous bread basket would be on the table, and even the most dedicated dieter would be powerless to resist.

Patricia's idea for a cake was wonderful, and she assured the future bride that she would be more than pleased with the final result. As a renowned pastry chef, she seemed to know exactly what Diane wanted, and her suggestions were met with enthusiasm by both of them. She settled on an almond cake with a meringue base frosted in buttercream, to be served with a raspberry coulis.

Patricia promised she would also bake her famous macaroons for the table that made such a hit with Peter when they had their recent dinner. Patricia returned to the kitchen, and they decided to eat lunch before going back to work. Benny Dalton walked through the dining room and came over to say hello to them.

"I understand I'll be supervising the preparation of your wedding luncheon, Mrs. Andrews. Patricia just advised me of your choices, and I applaud the selections. It will be a delicious, harmonious meal, and I'll personally be cooking the veal and cannelloni. Let me take the opportunity to congratulate you on your upcoming marriage." He shook Diane's hand, waved at Veronica, then walked to the rear of the room.

"He seems like such a nice guy," observed Diane, "not to mention good looking too."

"He is. It's hard to believe that someone attacked him at The Helping Hand only a few weeks ago."

"Have the police found out who did it yet?"

"I don't think so, but he appears to have moved on."

"Look, Diane," whispered Veronica presently, "doesn't it seem like Benny and Patricia are getting rather cozy?"

They glanced over to see both chefs leaning over a table reading from a clipboard, Benny's hand casually winding around Patricia's waist. She looked at him with a lingering glance, and they walked back to the kitchen together.

"Office romance, do you think?" asked Diane.

"Sure looks that way," said Veronica.

Chapter 28

The FBI drug task force meeting brought home the urgency to stem the tide of illegal drugs. Harry was aware that plans were being made to step up surveillance of plane drops. The information Peter Parelli was feeding him was going to make the job of putting Silvio out of business a lot easier. Peter had gotten word to Harry that the boat was due to leave Gloucester early tomorrow morning, using the same route as before and using the same drop method to get the packets of cocaine on the boat.

Peter assured Diane that this would be the last trip he would be taking before their wedding, scheduled in three weeks. She wanted him to take some time off to help prepare for their honeymoon cruise to Nassau.

"Couldn't we just take a train somewhere, sweetheart, or fly down to Florida?" he said.

"You just can't stand the idea that someone else will be the captain of the ship, Peter. We've already decided on a cruise, and I booked it this morning." He couldn't bear the look of disappointment on her face, so he smiled and kissed her and said a busman's holiday wouldn't be too bad after all.

For some reason, he was nervous about this trip, even though he knew it would be the last he would work for Silvio. Once this major drug bust took place, he would be out from under the man's thumb for good, so it was with anticipation that he left Diane's apartment for the waterfront this morning. He always felt good checking out the *Amanda Jane* personally, and he was in the wheelhouse as his crew turned up, one by one.

"Morning, Skipper," chirped Joe Flaherty, always the first to arrive. "Had to drag myself away from my kid this morning."

"How old is Joey now?"

"Three years old, and he's the cutest little guy. Lorraine bought him a captain's hat for his birthday two days ago, and he hasn't taken it off yet."

Shorty Rogers walked up the gangplank next, swinging his duffle bag. "Hi ya, Skip," he said with a big smile on his face.

"You're in a good mood for a change," observed Joe. "What's up?"

"My new girl, that's what's up. I hated to say goodbye to her this morning."

"Yes, I know what you mean," added Peter.

Corky Edwards came running down the dock and jumped up on the gangplank, closely followed by Tommy Quinlan. "Hey, Skipper, what's this I hear about you tying the knot again?" said Tommy.

"News gets around fast, I see. Yeah, guys, I was waiting until you all came aboard before I made my announcement."

Bruce Tucker sauntered up the walkway, then turned

toward the dock to wave at his wife and little girl. "Last but not least," said Peter, also waving to the small family standing together.

"What's this about an announcement?" Bruce asked.

"Now that you're all here, I want to tell you that I've decided to remarry, and this will be my last trip for a while. Diane and I will be going on a cruise for our honeymoon so I won't be back for about a month."

They all hooted and whistled at his news, and Peter thanked them.

"Diane is a wonderful woman; she's the head librarian over in Bromfield, and you'll all have a chance to meet her soon, I hope. Of course, if any of you guys ever decide to read a book, you can always introduce yourselves in person." His words were met with good-humored catcalls.

It was time to get underway. They pulled up anchor and cleared the port, heading out to sea under an overcast sky due to change to partly sunny soon. The sound of screeching seagulls circling the waterfront in the cool autumn wind was the perfect background noise to the ears of a commercial fisherman.

There was always something exciting about starting a new job . . . the anticipation of the open sea and whatever Mother Nature chose to throw at you . . . and you had better be ready for the challenge. Man against fish, that was the job, and the rolling sea under your feet was either going to be with you or against you.

Peter breathed deeply and looked for signs of change in the weather. He had given Harry the coordinates the FBI would use to intercept the airplane when they made the drop, and hopefully, the sea wasn't going to be too choppy.

He felt bad about his crew. They were good guys who were hardworking fishermen, and he would do whatever he could to get them off with a lighter sentence. They were aware they were being paid very well for smuggling illegal drugs. It was their choice, just as it was his, only in his case, he was the mole. He would deal with all of that later; he just wanted to concentrate on putting Silvio out of business for good.

Chapter 29

Benny had a lot to think about. His interview with Lieutenant Balducci took him off the list of suspects for Vickers's death. They knew he was working here at the soup kitchen on the night in question. Yet, they needed to double-check and remove him as a person of interest. On the other hand, they still had no one in custody yet for the attack on him, and he wondered if they would ever catch the man. It had only recently dawned on him that there could be a tie-in between the attack on him and the death of Robert Vickers, but he couldn't, for the life of him, figure out what it was. He would have to ask Patricia about it, but what would she know, he wondered.

He absentmindedly started to dice some vegetables. Somehow the repetitive movements of chopping always seemed to calm him down. He knew that only a professional chef would feel that way and smiled.

"Hi, Chef," said Karen Little, and he turned to face her. "A penny for your thoughts?" she asked.

"I'm not sure they are even worth a cent, but thanks for asking."

He looked at her again. Her freshly scrubbed face and ponytail made her look like a teenager, but he knew she was in her early thirties when she confided to him once and found they shared the same birth month. He observed, not for the first time, how pleasant she always seemed to be, but unlike him, upbeat. She was naturally pretty and always had a smell of fresh strawberries about her. Maybe it was the shampoo she used. Whatever it was, she always smelled nice. Why can't I fall for a nice woman like her, he wondered, somebody with no baggage, someone who's really interested in what I think and what I say?

Karen hesitated, and when Benny continued his chopping, she moved to the sink and started filling the stockpots with water.

On a whim, Benny turned to her. "I'm sorry if I seem preoccupied today, Karen. Tell me, how are things with you?"

"I was thinking of reapplying for work at Poppies, Chef. I heard through the grapevine that they are looking for prep chefs."

Benny registered surprise. "I had no idea Patricia wanted to hire someone. She never mentioned anything to me."

"Well, to tell you the truth, I could use the extra income. I'm taking some courses and want to earn a degree in food science at the community college."

"Yes, I remember you mentioned that. If you'd like, I would be more than happy to speak to Patricia on your behalf. I'm sure she wouldn't hold one of Robert's many tirades against you."

"That would be great. My car needs repairs, and I can use the money for that too."

"If you ever needed a ride to come here to the soup kitchen, just let me know, and I'll pick you up." The suddenness of his offer surprised even himself.

"Why, thanks," she said. "I may just take you up on that."

He went back to chopping, and soon, he started to whistle a tune. She turned back to the sink with a big smile on her face.

Tonight was Chicken à la King Night at The Helping Hand, second in popularity only to Meatloaf Night. Soon, the savory smells of sautéing onions, peppers, and spices filled the kitchen. The soup this evening was minestrone, and Karen was in charge of preparing it. The two chefs worked side by side, exchanging jokes as they cooked. A local restaurant had donated a large quantity of premixed dough, and the stoves were soon going full force, baking trays of hot biscuits to go with the chicken. Desserts always varied, depending on donations, and tonight, sweet rolls, cookies, and donuts were on the menu.

When they were through in the kitchen, Karen and Benny stood side by side sipping coffee, looking out at the sea of satisfied diners in the room.

"Do you ever wonder if they would eat at all if they couldn't come here for a meal?" asked Karen.

"I know exactly what it feels like because I was once in their position," said Benny.

Karen looked at him and wondered what other secrets he kept to himself. "I had no idea, Chef."

He found himself confiding his past life to her, how he felt about his family, and how much he had to endure to be his own person. Suddenly, she found herself telling him her story: about her privileged life as the only child of a wealthy family whose autocratic parents had mapped out her future without asking her if she wanted to go along with their plans.

Benny listened and realized that Karen had gone through almost the same tribulations and heartaches as he had. Her background was like his, and so was her resolve to change her life.

"Would you like to go for a drink after we clean up?" he asked suddenly. "I mean, it wouldn't have to be anywhere fancy; we're not really dressed for it."

"I would love to, Chef. I just have to put the pots and pans away first."

"Here, let me help you with that, and call me Benny. We can take my car, and I'll drop you back here afterward."

They went to an Italian restaurant not far from The Helping Hand, a quiet little place that served good food and had a liquor license. They ordered a bottle of wine to accompany the linguine with clam sauce and relished the opportunity to have someone else wait on them.

"I'm really enjoying this. Just the right amount of spices," said Benny. She nodded her agreement, and they toasted the meal by ordering more wine.

Karen was surprised to hear that Benny's background was very similar to her own. They were both brought up in families that had inherited money from generations before, and both felt like outsiders within their own social circle. They were the children of overbearing parents and found they liked classical music. They had both taken piano lessons as children. Karen loved to read, and so did Benny. They realized that they each were determined to take on life using their own set of rules and had little time for fools or people whom they considered their intellectual inferiors.

When the coffee and Sambuca cordial arrived, they sipped in companionable silence, each very comfortable with the other. The waiter presented the bill, and they reluctantly got up to leave. Benny drove Karen back to the now-darkened soup kitchen parking lot, her car the only one left.

"Thanks for a very nice evening, Benny. I'm glad we had the chance to get to know each other, and I hope we can do this again soon."

He stared at her wordlessly, and she could feel her heartbeat quicken from his steady gaze. Suddenly, he pulled her to him and kissed her with an intensity that took her breath away. When they parted, he mumbled, "Yes, very soon," and opened the car door.

Benny watched her drive away and wondered what had just happened to him. He realized that this woman was special and that he wanted to see her again. He was happy in her company, and suddenly, he realized he wanted her to be a part of his life.

Chapter 30

Veronica was busy doing inventory paperwork when she heard the bell over the door ring. Joe Banks had just left after his morning visit. She looked up to see Patricia Vickers standing in the doorway.

"How nice to see you, Mrs. Vickers," she said. "How may I help you today?"

"Call me Patricia, please. I wanted to see your store and had some time this morning before I had to be at the restaurant." She walked over to the jewelry cases and peered in. "I love antique jewelry and was told you had a good inventory." She pointed to a ring and asked to see it.

"This piece is a golden citrine and rose-cut diamond ring from the 1930s," said Veronica, placing it on the black velvet mat on top of the case. "It's set in platinum, and I particularly like the flower and trellis design detail around the sides."

Patricia examined the ring closely, then put it on her finger. "This is quite lovely. It's graceful and elegant at the same time, and citrine, or topaz, is my birthstone."

"It's mine as well," said Veronica.

Patricia looked up. "You're a Scorpio too?"

"I am," said Veronica.

"Ah, we are very loyal people, to be sure, but at the same time, we are not to be trifled with, don't you think?"

"I would say that is a fair assessment," smiled Veronica.

"I like the look of this on my hand. It's not so large that it can't be worn every day. I think I'll take it. I need to treat myself to something lovely. Let me look around and see if there's anything else," and she walked to the rear of the store to look at evening clothes.

The bell over the door rang again, and another woman came in. Veronica was surprised to see Karen Little from The Helping Hand.

"Good morning, Karen. I'm glad to meet you again. Let me know if I can help you find anything."

"I wanted to see your shop, Miss Howard. Everyone says it's a great place to find unusual vintage." She walked over to the jewelry case where Veronica was standing, then noticed Patricia Vickers coming toward her.

"Why, Mrs. Vickers," she said, "what a coincidence. I was planning to go over to the restaurant this morning and apply for the open position."

Patricia held out her hand. "You look familiar. Have we met before?"

"I'm Karen Little, and I'm a volunteer chef at The Helping Hand. Benny Dalton is a friend, and he suggested I come to see you."

The two women looked each other over.

"Do you have experience in a busy kitchen?" asked Patricia.

"Yes, I have, and I can show you my detailed résumé."

Patricia glanced at her wristwatch. "I should be at Poppies in about two hours. Come by and see me then, and we'll talk some more."

"Thank you. I'll do that." Karen realized her brief work experience at Poppies before Robert fired her for not chopping the vegetables to his standards would have to be discussed. Strangely enough, Patricia had not worked that day. Maybe Benny's influence would convince Patricia to give her another chance.

Patricia opened her checkbook, and Veronica handed her the ring box.

"I'm so pleased I found this lovely piece. I'll be back again when I have more time to shop." She waved and walked out the door.

Karen walked over to the window and watched Patricia drive away and wondered if fate had placed her here this morning. She was aware that there was a certain undercurrent when they talked but couldn't understand what it was. Everyone always said that the late Robert Vickers could be intimidating, and she certainly knew that from her own experience working in his kitchen. But now, she felt that Patricia imparted the same feeling and wondered if she could work for someone that made her feel even slightly uncomfortable. Well, beggars can't be choosers, and she decided to override her feelings and go ahead with the interview.

"Are you all right, Karen?" said Veronica.

"Oh yes, I'm just daydreaming."

"I know Patricia Vickers can be rather intimidating sometimes."

Karen looked up. "How perceptive you are. I was just

thinking the same thing."

"I had an occasion to spend some time with her recently while helping a friend plan her wedding reception and found that she can be quite kind. I'm sure you will see that side of her too. I understand she had a lot to deal with as her late husband's personality could be overwhelming at times. But she couldn't have been nicer to my friend and me too, for that matter."

"Benny feels the same way you do, but, then again, Benny tends to see what he wants to see."

Veronica nodded and wondered if there was more to her observation than met the eye.

After Karen left the store, she went back to her desk to finish some paperwork. For some reason, she was unable to concentrate, and it was about fifteen minutes later that she suddenly dropped her pen and sat still in her chair. The old familiar feeling was coming over her . . . the chill down her spine from her "second sight" that always seemed to predict danger. The question was . . . What were the circumstances, and who was it going to affect this time?

Chapter 31

Diane was missing Peter as she glanced down at her new engagement ring. They had decided to exchange simple bands when they took their wedding vows in a few weeks. Everything seemed to be coming together, and Diane momentarily crossed her fingers in the hope that her good luck would hold. Nothing is going to come between Peter and me, and our happiness will blot out all the awful memories of my miserable marriage to Carl. Once again, she thanked her lucky stars she had found a man who would finally put her first. She knew in her heart that he was the love of her life, and she should always find a way to tell him that.

As a special wedding gift for her new husband, Diane found a beautifully bound antique book on the maritime history of Gloucester's port in a little out-of-the-way book shop near Bromfield. It was in excellent condition considering its age, and even though she had to dip into her savings to buy it, she knew he would treasure both the book and her thoughtfulness. She couldn't wait to see the look on Peter's face when he opened the package.

Diane had never been much of a cook, but given the fact

that she was marrying a man who fished for a living, she thought it was about time for her to learn how to prepare seafood. She started to borrow every cookbook the library had to compile recipes that she could make for him. She was busy looking over ingredients for a garlicky Mediterranean fish stew when the radio announcer interrupted the show she was listening to. He reported that the former Beatle, John Lennon, had just been shot outside his New York City apartment building for no apparent reason. Diane loved the Beatles and was shocked to hear that something like that could happen in this day and age. We certainly live in dangerous times, she thought, when someone so famous could have his life snuffed out in a matter of moments.

She thought she would probably die if anyone shot her Peter, then silently admonished herself for her foolishness because she knew, of course, that was never going to happen. She was just going to have to make sure to kill him with love and good fish dinners, and he would be all right. When he came back from this current trip to sea, and they went on their honeymoon, their new life together would officially start, and she would finally be content and happy in married life.

Veronica called Diane to remind her that her engagement party tonight was being held at 7:00 rather than at 6:00 at the Bromfield Tea Room to allow extra rush-hour time for those women who had to travel there from work. Diane had always loved the old-fashioned feel of the tearoom, where each table had a different place setting. It was a cozy and eclectic place with a strong Victorian flavor, kind of fussy for Veronica's taste, but the food and service were excellent, and she knew Diane would enjoy the atmosphere. She had asked a small group of women to attend, mostly coworkers at the library and two distant cousins that Diane still kept in touch with.

They sat at a table set up in a private room with a lilacs-and-roses theme in wallpaper and décor. The colorful wrapping paper of the gifts was reflected in the large mirror over a fireplace lit on this chilly evening, making it especially festive. The buffet table held heated serving dishes of beef stroganoff, curried chicken, rice, salad, and the house specialty of fresh popover rolls. The sounds of laughter became louder as the consumption of champagne and cocktails increased.

Veronica was pleased that Diane had received presents that were truly meaningful to an older bride. She already had household appliances and items one would typically gift to a first-time wife. These friends all knew Diane's circumstances and were truly happy she would be starting married life again with a more suitable husband. The gifts reflected the current trend for luxury items, plus a few saucy pieces of underwear that brought titters of laughter when she opened them. Not everyone had met Peter, but they knew he was a romantic man who had swept their friend off her feet.

When Diane opened Veronica's gift, though, her eyes started to tear. It was a large, ornate sterling silver frame bearing the photo of a happy Peter and Diane smiling at each other, taken on the night they had gone out to dinner with Harry and Veronica. Attached was an envelope containing a gift certificate to a resort for a special spa weekend for couples only. Diane hugged her and thanked her profusely.

"When you try to talk Peter into retirement again," giggled Veronica, "make sure you do it while he's lying on his stomach on a massage table. He will be so relaxed that he won't dare to argue with you."

Chapter 32

The sea this early in the morning was relatively calm past Portsmouth and the New Hampshire coastline up toward Maine and eventually holding all the way up to the Maritimes, just as the National Weather Bureau had predicted. The *Amanda Jane*'s wooden hull had recently undergone an overhaul, and the big engines hummed smoothly, the background noise of it accompanying the crew through their routine tasks of running a large fishing vessel.

The sun was warm, and its reflection on the water and the salt air was like a tonic to the men, who breathed it for a living. But they knew from experience that the now serene and tranquil water could turn on them faster than a woman scorned. Peter checked the nautical charts. His mind was really focused on his future bride and how Diane would describe her engagement party's details, which she would reveal to him at great length. He smiled at the thought and silently pinched himself at how lucky he was finally to be marrying this wonderful lady.

Soon enough, though, he knew that because he revealed the coordinates of this last trip to Harry and the FBI, his boat would soon be boarded, and the crew arrested and charged with smuggling and several other serious indictments. He would go through the charade of being arrested too but would ultimately be cleared for his pivotal role in helping to bring down the drug empire of Aldo Silvio.

He had agonized daily over his actions, but, in the end, the memory of his beloved brother's sad death and his hatred of Silvio and everything he stood for was propelling him forward. When he got back to shore after this trip, he would reveal all to Diane and hoped she would understand his motivation. He was gambling that she would forgive him for the lies he had told her and for placing her in danger as well.

But first, they had to catch some fish. It would be another ten hours or so before they would throw out the nets, and he would not deviate from any action he would generally take on any other trip. It pained him to listen to his crew talking happily among themselves about what they were going to do with their pay and how they were missing their women and children.

When they finally realized it was their trusted skipper, Peter Parelli, who had betrayed them, he knew the inevitable hatred in their eyes would stay in his memory forever. After all, he hired this crew, and they looked upon him as their boss and hero. They would never be able to pull down the money they were making aboard the *Amanda Jane* with any other skipper. Drug money was dirty in more ways than one. It propped up weak men, and it enabled their dreams to be built on quicksand. The fast buck became their god, and the faster they made it, the quicker they would spend it.

Peter had discussed his fears at length with Harry. He

had decided to expose his feelings to a man who made his living not from the sea like himself, but from conclusions made while sitting behind a desk. Perhaps that's why he trusted Harry, whose calm demeanor and quiet nature made it easy for him to talk about the things that bothered him.

He realized that Harry's personality was so different from his own. As an Italian-American man, he was passionate and outspoken about the things he cared about—his job, his responsibilities, and the things that mattered to him. It was just that he was propelled by self-loathing and guilt because he could never convince his own brother to give up drugs.

Peter recognized that Harry was a passionate man too, only his passion was for culture and excellence in the arts. Harry was also an employer, responsible for other people's lives with a duty to those who trusted him to make the right decisions for their welfare. And he cared deeply for Veronica; that was plain to see. Peter finally concluded that the only difference between himself and Harry was that Harry went about his job wearing a three-piece suit. He wore a yellow oilskin sou'wester over an old woolen sweater and blue jeans.

Harry's hands were not calloused like his were, but his heart and head were just as focused on the end game. Both men sought justice in his own way and in his own time, and this time, fate had thrown them together . . . the undercover FBI Special Agent and the fishing boat captain-turned-informant, now seeking retribution.

Peter knew that Harry's bond with Veronica meant as much to him as his with Diane. He concluded that they would both do just about anything to keep their women happy. He had shared his feelings with Harry over a drink.

"I see what a great relationship you and Veronica have, and I applaud you both for living your lives the way you want to."

"It didn't happen overnight, Peter. But I pretty much knew right away that Veronica was the woman for me. She was the first relationship I ever had that I considered I had found my soul mate. I know those words are bandied about a lot lately, but I can honestly say we have a true meeting of the minds, despite our different temperaments on occasion."

"You can't always agree with the person you love," said Peter.

"That's true, but if you put the person you love first and tell them so regularly, life is easier, believe me."

They both agreed, and both laughed that it took them some time to absorb and act on this wisdom.

Chapter 33

Karen entered Poppies by the kitchen door and saw Patricia concentrating on kneading dough. Presently, she looked up, smiled, washed her hands, and motioned to Karen to follow her into the office and closed the door. Karen presented her résumé and studied the woman closely as she read it.

"I see you've had quite a bit of experience in food prep. I wasn't aware that you had worked in this kitchen for a short time, either."

"It seemed that the way I cut the vegetables wasn't to your late husband's liking. He never gave me a chance to do it his way, and I believe you were away taking a course out of town when he hired—and fired—me."

The two women stared at each other. Finally, Patricia smiled.

"I suppose I should apologize for Robert. He had appalling temper tantrums, and it took all my energy sometimes just to keep a staff. I'm happy to say that things have changed for the better with Benny Dalton on board. Oh yes, I believe you told me you know him."

"Yes, I do, and a more qualified head chef would be pretty hard to find, I would imagine," said Karen.

"I see you excelled in your courses at culinary school. What kinds of things do you like to cook?"

"I'm pretty much about keeping food honest and fresh. I like to enhance natural flavors lightly but also like to experiment with textures. Masking dishes with heavy sauces and gravies is not my thing."

"It sounds like we share the same aesthetic. We espouse nouvelle cuisine here but not to the point of being minimalistic. I want my patrons to be presented with more than an artistically placed lettuce leaf and a daub of dressing. Believe me, I wouldn't be in business long if I served what some of my detractors and competitors pass off as 'fine dining.'"

"Forgive me, Mrs. Vickers, but who could possibly think to fault your wonderful menu? What I mean is that I know the quality of the product you offer, and only a stupid Philistine with no taste buds would think to complain."

Patricia laughed with gusto. "Thanks for the compliment, and I must say, you sound just like Benny. That's definitely something he would yell to some poor, unsuspecting diner who would never see it coming because he's never been afraid to speak his mind. Do you know Benny well?"

"Does anyone really know Benny well, Mrs. Vickers?"

Touché, thought Patricia. This girl seems to have it together. I wonder if she's one of the legions of women who find Benny irresistible . . . including me. Should I hire her and find out?

"That's a fair observation." What the hell, she thought, let me give her a shot.

"I pay well and will expect your best efforts every day. We are a team here, as you already know. But I always have the last word because my reputation is on the line with every dish I serve. Would you have a problem with that?"

"Fair is what I like, Mrs. Vickers. All I ask is that if you ever have a problem with my work, you tell me and give me a chance to make it right."

"Call me Patricia, and I'm not my late husband, Karen. When can you start?"

The office door opened just as Benny was coming out of the walk-in freezer. He looked at Patricia's smiling face, then Karen, and wondered if this was going to be double trouble for him.

"Karen will be joining our staff as of tomorrow, Benny. I appreciate that you recommended her, and I look forward to a long and productive relationship."

Benny grinned from ear to ear. "Welcome aboard, Karen. I'll walk you out to your car."

The phone rang in the office, and Patricia ran to answer it. That will be Aldo, she thought, letting me know about the next delivery.

Benny opened the car door. "Well, that was painless," said Karen. "She was quite nice to me, actually."

"She is nice, very nice," said Benny.

The way he said it made Karen think that Benny had a soft spot for her. Or was it more?

"I'm working late tonight, but I'll buy you a drink afterward to celebrate," he said.

She squeezed his hand. "I'd better not, Benny. I want to be my best for tomorrow morning. Funny, but I feel like a grammar school kid on her way to the first day in the classroom."

"I understand. We'll do it another time soon. I'll see you tomorrow then, and congratulations." He waved as she drove out of the parking lot.

It hadn't dawned on him yet that this new turn of events would cause him great anxiety . . . and worse.

Chapter 34

Veronica woke up a little after midnight from a bad dream. It wasn't often she experienced night sweating and anxiety. It only seemed to happen when her second sight warned her that an unsettling event was about to happen. She got out of bed and walked into her small kitchen and made a cup of herbal tea. There would be no getting back to sleep, so she gave in and settled on her living room sofa with a notebook, the tea, and her harlequin glasses.

Much of her time in the past week was taken up with Diane and her wedding plans. But Veronica just couldn't shake the idea that something sinister was about to happen. She jotted down events in their sequence and realized that Benny and Patricia both figured strongly in Diane's wedding story.

Peter Parelli, she felt, just wasn't everything he seemed. She liked him very much, and he appeared to be the perfect man for Diane, but something nagged at her that there was more to him than he let on. She would have to ask Harry this morning what he thought about that. Harry was her sounding board and usually had an opinion to share.

She wondered why Benny's attacker wasn't in custody yet and why that investigation seemed to have stalled. Was it because Benny and Patricia worked together the reason why Robert Vickers was murdered and Benny attacked?

What about the murder of Violet Thompson's son? Was there a connection between Kevin Thompson, drugs, and the Vickers?

There seemed to be a common theme to all these events. Somehow, they were tied in together. But right now, she couldn't for the life of her figure it out. She just knew that something evil was going to happen to someone she knew, and she needed to stop it.

Suddenly, a deep sadness overcame her. She closed her eyes and curled up on the sofa, exhausted from her mental efforts, and fell into a deep sleep. She woke up as the morning sun streamed through the bow window. Birds were chirping outside as she glanced at the carriage clock on the sofa table. Veronica realized she had been sleeping there for over five hours. She hurried to take a shower and get ready for work.

Chapter 35

The sonar bleeps told Peter that a large school of fish was right under the boat. He yelled to the men and they sprang into action, each doing his job in the time-honored tradition of a fisherman. The big nets fanned out over the water, and the catch was going to be a good one. The crew whooped and hollered as they hauled up the lines. Full nets translated into profits, and money was what it was all about.

Peter consulted the charts and realized the boat was about an hour from the plane's drop-off point. But first things first. The catch had to be gutted and cleaned except for the whole fish that would house the drug parcels that would eventually be delivered to Poppies Restaurant. It was business as usual onboard the *Amanda Jane*.

The weather was holding up, and the sea was calm. Under ordinary circumstances, Peter would be elated, but now, he was nervous and jumpy. He didn't want anything to get in the way of this sting. The price he was going to pay was high, but he knew it was the right thing for him to do. Those bastards were going to pay for the addiction of the countless victims caught in the web of drugs. They were like the fish he was hauling into the net . . . helpless to fight their fate and unable to swim away.

The ice room had been churning out chips all morning in preparation for such a catch. The men donned their boots, slickers, and gloves and cut and sliced their way through the filled buckets of squirming fish. There was a primeval rhythm to their movements; man and fish working their way through their karma.

By midafternoon, the crew was ready to rest and eat. They were exhausted, but everyone was in a good mood. Peter cut the engines and waited for the seaplane to land. It usually took about ten minutes for a drop to be made.

The routine was always the same. The plane would land next to the boat, and the pilot and a helper would push the flotation boxes out of the cabin into the water, and the crew would retrieve and load them on board the *Amanda Jane*. Peter was told to expect a larger shipment this trip.

When all the boxes were loaded, the crew would haul them down to the ice room and fill the fish with the individual parcels. Peter always supervised this step personally at Silvio's request, but he knew that would not be the case this time.

Presently, he could hear the hum of an airplane. He strained his eyes, looking for it. Right on time, as usual, he thought. Peter made sure the cabinet under the wheel that housed two pistols was unlocked, the keys safely in his pocket. The plane swooped down onto the water like a large silver bird. The pilot came out and stood on the fixed wing and waved to Peter. The copilot joined him and stretched his back in the warming sun. The crew of the *Amanda Jane*, grappling hooks in hand, was poised to retrieve the cargo and haul it aboard.

Suddenly, they heard the sound of another, larger plane, and all heads swiveled in its direction. The pilot and copilot looked at each other and scrambled back inside the cockpit, caught off guard by the arrival of this second aircraft. The pilot started the engine, and the propellers coughed into action, but not before three skydivers landed between his plane and the boat. The larger plane dropped down in front of them, preventing their takeoff.

Peter had taken the precaution of emptying the bullets from the guns beforehand, so it was a hollow gesture when he appeared on deck brandishing one. He had to make a show of fending off this surprise ambush at the request of the authorities. He had to be seen defending the cargo.

Fortunately, the pilot and copilot didn't even have time to get off a shot from the rifles they kept in the cockpit. They saw it was futile to fight. Their plane was boarded, and they were arrested immediately. A US Coast Guard cutter soon came into view, and armed officers boarded the *Amanda Jane*, arresting Peter and the crew.

Chapter 36

The whole sting operation took less than half an hour. The FBI gave all participants strict instructions that Peter was to be treated like the others for appearance's sake. When the flotilla arrived back in Gloucester, he was taken into custody and processed through the criminal system, along with the rest of his crew. It was understood that his undercover status would be preserved, even though he had given explicit instructions to the authorities that this would be his last job. He would soon be reunited with Diane, but not before Silvio was arrested and jailed.

Peter gave Harry the task to inform Diane of the situation, and he was not looking forward to it. He did the only thing he could think of and asked Veronica to go with him.

"Harry, how could you let this happen?" she cried. "How do you think that poor girl is going to react when she hears the Drug Enforcement Agency has arrested her soon-to-be new husband?"

"We'll soon find out, Veronica. That's why you're here, to give Diane moral support."

"What can I possibly say to her to make her feel good about this?"

"Why don't you just leave that part to me?"

Veronica called Diane at the library and asked her to meet her at the store for lunch. When she walked in and saw Harry, she ran over to him and kissed his cheek. Then she saw the serious looks on their faces and asked if anything was wrong. Veronica led her into the stockroom, where they all sat down. Susan was waiting on customers and was told not to disturb them under any circumstances.

When they were seated, Harry took Diane's hand.

"Harry, what's wrong? Has anything happened to Peter?"

"Peter is fine, Diane, but I have a long story to tell you." He proceeded to recount what happened while she sat as still as a statue.

When he had done, tears rolled down her cheeks. "Why couldn't he tell me any of it? I should have been hearing this from Peter, not from you, Harry."

"He couldn't tell you any more than I could tell Veronica about my part in all this. We were working undercover, Diane. Our lives depend on silence. Do you understand?"

Veronica went over to Diane, and the two women hugged each other.

"The important thing is that Peter is all right. He asked me to explain the situation to you because his part in this is not over yet. He has to pretend to be a drug smuggler until the authorities arrest Aldo Silvio."

"You mean he has to spend time in jail? Like a common criminal?"

"It's all for show, Diane," explained Harry. "He took the

biggest risk in giving us the exact position of the drug drop. He pretended to go along with Silvio to avenge his brother's death, who died from overdosing on drugs. It was important for him to do this, to avenge his brother's death."

"Why couldn't he tell me all this himself?" she asked again.

"He did it for your safety. He didn't want to drag you into this any more than he had to."

"But he did, Harry; he did drag me into this when he asked me to marry him. And he did it without my knowledge and consent."

Harry looked at Veronica and shrugged.

Veronica spoke up. "Harry, you have to understand where Diane is coming from. She is marrying a man that she not only has given her heart to but her trust as well. You know her relationship with Carl was built on lies and deceit, and she has never really gotten over the breakdown in communication it caused between them. It ultimately destroyed their marriage."

Diane nodded her head sadly. "What about our wedding? I suppose I will have to call it off now."

"I don't think that will be necessary, Diane," said Harry. "Peter will be released by the authorities very soon—as soon as they arrest Silvio. He just must play this out and go through with the fiction of not knowing anything about the sting. Nothing will change—not your plans or anything else."

"You're wrong, Harry," said Diane. "*Everything* has changed. I've been deliberately left out of the most important decision Peter will probably ever make in his life. Safety issues aside, I don't know how I'm going to be able to get past that."

Veronica stood up, went over to a cabinet, took out a bottle of brandy, poured out three glasses, and handed them around. Diane refused hers, but Veronica pushed it into her hands.

"For medicinal purposes, my dear friend," she urged. "Please drink it." They all sipped in silence.

"Peter will be calling you tonight," said Harry presently. "He wanted me to be sure you know that. He loves you and wants to tell you everything."

Diane shook her head. "It may be too late for that."

"Please promise me you will listen to everything he has to say," said Veronica. "He's a brave man to take on an entire drug cartel . . . stupid maybe, but extremely brave. And as for you, Harry Hunt, you and I are going to have a serious talk as well because you were a big part of all this."

"The funny thing is that Peter and I never realized the other was an undercover agent until the night we all went to dinner at Poppies. We had a brief meeting the week before to exchange information about the sting, but that night, when we realized the truth about each other's involvement, we couldn't reveal our identities to those we cared the most about."

"Is that supposed to make us feel better?" asked Veronica.

"Yes!" said Harry with feeling. "Yes, you're supposed to feel secure in the fact that what we do in our jobs has nothing at all to do with how we feel about the women we love."

Veronica nodded her head sadly.

"That's the big difference between men and women, in a nutshell, Harry. Men will almost always put their jobs first before their personal lives."

Diane got up from the chair and handed her empty glass to Veronica. "I'll call you tomorrow, Ronnie. Thank you for being here for me, and thank you too, Harry, for having the courage to tell me the truth. Maybe things will look better to me then, but right now, I'm not so sure." She kissed them both and walked dejectedly out of the store.

Chapter 37

Patricia had been trying to reach Aldo on the phone all night. The fish and drugs should have arrived by now, and she had been keeping the two dealers hanging around to help unload them into the walk-in freezer. Now that Kevin Thompson was out of the picture, the others were grumbling about the extra work they were expected to do.

She would have to look into a replacement first thing tomorrow. She liked to keep the personnel numbers small for control purposes. But for now, she needed to count the bags to make sure they were on the street for sale tomorrow morning. She wondered what could be stalling the delivery. Everyone knew how important timing was, that fish were fragile and quickly decay. Patricia would have to make sure they thawed out slowly so that they wouldn't be ruined for the restaurant menu. Not for the first time she asked if she had to do everything herself.

She went into the office and tried Aldo's phone number once again . . . with no result. He had given her another number once to an emergency telephone that was only to be used as a last resort. She sat down at her desk, opened the middle drawer, and pulled out a tiny manicure kit. In a hidden pocket opposite the nail clippers was a piece of rolled-up paper. She smoothed it out and called the number written on it. After three rings, it was answered by a woman with an Italian accent.

"*Pronto.*"

"This is Patricia Vickers. I must speak to Mr. Silvio right away."

"Signor Silvio is not here. *Cosa vuoi?* What do you want?"

"I have a question that only he can answer, and it's important that I have that answer immediately," she said.

"*Non è possibile*—it is not possible for me to reach him now. I will tell him you called."

"Tell him it's an emergency. It's Mrs. Vickers."

"*Sì,* I will tell him, *signora,*" said the voice, and the phone call was abruptly disconnected.

I wonder if that's his wife, thought Patricia. Will she give him my message? If I don't hear from him in an hour, I'll have to send the men home and close the kitchen.

She was getting more anxious by the minute. She couldn't afford to have the drug operation close down. She needed it to continue to flourish so that the restaurant could stay open and Aldo to remain a silent partner. If he pulled out now, she wouldn't know what to do. It was up to her to keep things moving. If anything—or anyone—got in her way, she would have to deal with the situation herself. She suspected that Aldo would respect her more if she took more of an active role in his operation. In fact, she reasoned, he probably needed her as much as she needed him. He's given me the scope and leeway to keep things on an even keel, and I *must* do that.

Whenever Patricia felt anxious or distraught, the only thing that calmed her was baking. She went back to the kitchen and decided to make some bread. The two dealers sat down in a corner with a deck of cards and waited. A few minutes later the kitchen door opened and Benny walked in. Patricia looked up in surprise.

"Benny? What are you doing here at this hour?"

He looked over at the two men. "I could ask you the same question. I was driving by and saw your car in the lot, plus a pickup truck I didn't recognize. Who are they? Is there something wrong?"

"Oh no," she laughed. "Nothing's wrong. I had to clear up some paperwork, and these fellows came by looking for kitchen jobs." She turned to the two men. "I'm sorry, but there's no work for you just now. Tell Mr. Silvio I'll be in touch with him if I need you. Good night."

They put the cards away and walked out without saying a word. Benny locked the door behind them. "What's going on here, Patricia?"

She brushed a lock of hair out of her eyes. "Nothing's going on, Benny. I told you."

He glanced at his wristwatch. "It's almost three in the morning."

"I know what time it is. I have a watch too." He walked over to her and took her in his arms.

She rudely pushed him away. "Are you stalking me, Benny? What are you really doing here at this hour?"

"I worked a double shift at The Helping Hand and then went out for a couple of beers with some of the other volunteers. I was still feeling restless and drove down to the waterfront, then took the shore road home when I saw your car in the lot, as I told you."

She continued to glare at him without saying a word.

He was hurt and confused. "You know, I do have better things to do than to stalk you, Patricia," he sneered. He turned around abruptly and slammed the door on his way out.

Benny sat behind the wheel of his car in the darkened parking lot and breathed slowly in and out to gain control of his temper. He didn't like what was going on with Patricia and felt helpless because she was pushing him away. If she were in any trouble at all, he hoped she would at least confide in him. It seemed she had a champion in this Silvio, but in the short time that she had known this man, he definitely could feel a change in his relationship with Patricia.

Maybe the rumors were right; perhaps he is a major player in drugs. He certainly didn't look the part. His sleek and polished persona and the calming influence he had on Patricia couldn't be denied. She had told Benny that Aldo Silvio was her new legal counsel and helped her sort out the paperwork mess and some debts that Robert had left behind.

Benny also knew that Poppies was currently making money due largely to his running the kitchen in a profitable manner. Despite the extensive publicity of a death occurring on-site, people were booking reservations, not out of curiosity but because the restaurant's reputation was not tarnished. Good food and service always won out in the end.

He suspected that Patricia was romantically involved with this Mr. Silvio and hoped she wasn't trying to edge him out of his job because she may have feelings for him as well.

Because when it came down to it, and if he were honest with himself, his job meant more to him than having a fling with Patricia Vickers. However, his interest in Karen Little had now become more than a light flirtation, and he knew she felt the same about him. It still bothered him, though, that Patricia couldn't at least be honest enough with him and let him know what was going on.

He started the car and noticed the lights in the kitchen had been turned off. Maybe Patricia was going to spend the night on the sofa bed in the office. He hesitated a moment, then stepped on the gas. He decided that he would confront her tomorrow and ask her again what was troubling her.

Patricia leaned on the desk and put both hands on it to stop herself from shaking. What's happening to me? I'm a nervous wreck. First, I can't get in touch with Aldo to find out what happened to the shipment; then I yell at Benny for no reason at all, and now I'm losing control over things that I need to do.

She splashed water on her face, shut off the desk lamp, locked the door, and activated the burglar alarm. The kitchen and all her problems would still be here in a few hours. Sleeping on the convertible bed in her office was not what she had planned on doing tonight, but until she heard from Aldo, there was no other option.

Chapter 38

Silvio never received the message his housekeeper took over the telephone from Patricia. He had been under surveillance for several months and was finally arrested at his home without incident. His calm demeanor remained intact in spite of being hauled in for questioning in the middle of the night. The authorities had worked hard to coordinate their efforts. Despite a judge-ordered warrant to search his residence, little or no incriminating evidence was found to keep him in custody longer than the standard forty-eight hours. The lawyer had himself hired a lawyer, one who was as familiar with mob arrests as he was.

It all came down to the testimony given by Peter Parelli. His word and the diary of events he had secretly record-ed would make all the difference in the prosecution's case against the slick attorney's operation.

The next morning, Harry was present when Peter was ushered into the office of the district attorney in Boston.

"How are you holding up, Peter?" asked Harry.

"I'll be happy when this is all over," he replied. "I'm satis-fied that I've done all I can do to put this *diavolo*, this 'devil,' behind bars for many years."

He received the officers' thanks and was told he would be placed under surveillance for his own protection.

Harry and Peter walked out and went into a little coffee shop near the State House. They sipped in silence, and then Harry asked the question.

"Have you figured out yet how you're going to tell Diane about this?"

"I think the only thing I can do is shoot straight from the hip. What I don't want to tell her is what I heard today—that I should strongly consider the Witness Protection Program for my and her own safety."

"I don't envy you, my friend. I can't imagine what Veronica would say if I had the same decision to make."

"I'm just going to be honest with her and tell her I want to buy my own boat, just as I always have wanted to do, retire in a few years, and live life happily ever after with her at my side."

"Keeping it simple is a good idea."

"Harry, what choice do I have? As far as Silvio's associates know, I've been arrested and will go to jail for my part in their drug operation. The FBI assured me that it would be all for show and they will soon release me on a 'technicality.' They are even willing to put a 'ringer' in jail who looks like me. I can then marry Diane quietly, keep a low profile, and then we can live our lives. Nothing will change except for the time frame."

"Veronica tells me that Diane is disappointed that you didn't tell her the truth about your plan."

"How could I tell her, Harry? The feds put a gag order on

me for my own and her protection. I was so close to the end of all this after the months of planning and couldn't take any chances. You understand that, don't you?"

"I understand, Peter; of course, I do. But the question is, will Diane understand?"

"I have to make her see that I had no choice. I can't lose the woman I love over this."

Chapter 39

It was midmorning when Patricia finally awoke after spending a restless night sleeping in the office. She ran into the small bathroom that she had insisted be installed when she and Robert had built the restaurant, then quickly showered and threw on yesterday's clothes.

She immediately redialed Aldo's phone number, and after a long wait, the same woman as last night answered.

"It's Patricia Vickers again. Can Mr. Silvio come to the phone and speak to me now?"

"Signore Silvio is not here. I know nothing about where he is."

"I need to talk to him now. He has to tell me what I'm to do next," she whined.

"When I see him I will ask him to call you, *signora*." And she hung up.

Patricia was beside herself. She knew she had to remain calm and carry on despite these irritating events. She knew that Aldo would not leave her hanging without some explanation. She could only conclude that something catastrophic had happened that he had to deal with, and it was up to her to keep a cool head and carry on. Yes, she felt she could handle whatever happened now in her own way. Until she heard from Aldo to the contrary, she was now in charge.

She decided to do what she always did when she was stressed, and that was to bake. She started the dough for her signature brioche rolls. She consulted her meal plan and saw that tarts would be on the menu that day, so she chose fresh peaches and pears from the pantry storeroom. Soon, the other employees would come in, and the kitchen would be humming again. She took a deep breath. Now, she knew where she was and calmly started kneading the dough.

Benny walked into the busy kitchen several hours later and saw Patricia putting sheet plans into the oven. He put on his white uniform and consulted the day's meal plan. The air was thick with tension.

Patricia spoke first. "Chef, could I see you in my office, please?"

Benny followed her in and closed the door. "Okay, Patricia, are you ready to tell me what's going on?"

She looked at him with a mixture of sadness and resolve. "There are things in my life that I have little or no control over at the moment, Benny. I'm sorry if I snapped at you, but I've got a lot on my mind right now."

He walked over to the sofa and sat down. "Okay, I get it. I thought we were friends. You know you can tell me anything, and it won't go any further than this room."

She smiled and sat down next to him. "Thanks for that; thanks for your loyalty, and I know you must be wondering what those men were doing here last night."

"I already know what they were doing here, Patricia. I

know more than you think. Would you like me to run down exactly what I know?"

His voice was no longer soft and mellow. He stood up and moved away from her.

"I know that Robert had huge gambling debts and was on the brink of losing this place. I also know that the mob offered a way out but not without extracting a pound of flesh. You played along, and the pound of flesh turned out to be yours."

Patricia leaped off the sofa and slapped him hard across the face.

"How dare you speak to me like that!" she cried. "I would have lost everything if Aldo Silvio hadn't come to my rescue. Robert had cut me out and treated me like a stranger. All my work would have come to nothing if Aldo hadn't taken over. I owe him everything."

The air was charged with electricity as they glared at each other. Finally, Benny broke the silence.

"Just when did you turn into a grubby little drug dealer, Patricia? The day you decided to play along with Silvio was the day you lost your integrity and your dream. I suspect he had Robert killed, and I'm guessing he sent someone to attack me, for what reason I'm not sure, and he will keep you dangling on a string for as long as it pleases him."

She started to cry, but he continued.

"Don't you realize I know all about the cocaine packets in the fish? I know those guys were here last night to get paid for pushing the stuff, and I'm also aware that another one of them was killed a few nights ago. He was getting sloppy and greedy and had to die before he spilled the beans."

"How do you know, Benny? Who told you?"

"Remember, I work at a soup kitchen, and I keep my eyes and ears open. People talk, Patricia, and I've been listening. I see things here at Poppies that don't add up to the stories you tell. Up to now, I've told no one what's going on, but I refuse to be dragged into a net when the police finally find out about your nasty little secret. And it's only a matter of time before they do find out."

"But . . . but I could lose everything," she spluttered. "I can't take that chance, and you can't tell anyone!"

She sat down quickly, picked up the phone with one hand, and opened the top drawer with the other.

"All I have to do is call Aldo now, and he'll take care of everything for me. I don't need to listen to your threats and innuendoes."

"Then why hasn't he gotten in touch with you, Patricia? You're distraught because this drug kingpin is leaving you out of the loop just like Robert did. They're users, these people. Don't you understand that yet?"

"Shut up, Benny . . . just shut up. You don't know what I'm going through, so just stay out of my way."

He started to walk over to her. She grabbed the gun from the drawer, pointed it at him, and squeezed the trigger.

His ears heard the sound, but his eyes followed the pain he felt in his shoulder, and he saw blood seeping through his white chef's jacket.

Patricia dropped the gun to the floor as if it were on fire and stood up, riveted to the spot.

The color drained from Benny's face as he turned and stumbled out the office door. One of the kitchen workers saw him and ran to help.

"Chef! You OK, Chef?"

"Quick, José," gasped Benny, "grab some clean towels and help me over to my desk."

He picked up the telephone, but Patricia ran over and grabbed it out of his hand. "Who are you calling?"

He moaned from the pain. "I'm losing blood. I need to call 911 Emergency."

"Get in the car, Benny. I'll drive you to the hospital."

She ordered her kitchen staff to carry on and said she would be back shortly, then asked José to help her get Benny into the front seat of her car.

Karen had just driven into the parking lot and saw that Benny was bleeding. She rushed over to help, but Patricia turned her away.

"Just a little accident with a knife, Karen," she said. "Do me a favor and see that the lunch service is covered. I'm driving Benny to the hospital now, and I'll call as soon as he's been stabilized. Don't worry about anything here. I've got it covered. Just don't tell anyone else about this. You understand?"

She stepped on the gas and tore out of the parking lot.

Karen ran into the kitchen and asked if anyone had seen what had happened. José was at the sink washing the blood from his hands and putting the wet towels into a plastic bag.

"Chef come out of the office holding his shoulder. I get these towels for him, and he bleeding a lot."

"But how did he get a cut on his shoulder from a knife, José?"

"We no see nothin', Miss Karen. We just hear a shot."

"*What?* Benny was *shot?* Who has a gun in here?"

"It come from the office, I think." And he pointed toward the baize door.

Karen rushed to the door that was still open and saw the gun on the floor next to Patricia's desk.

"Has anyone called the police yet?" she asked, then dialed the number herself.

Chapter 40

Diane was at her apartment when Peter called. He asked her to sit down and listen to what he had to say.

"I know you have many questions for me, my love, and I don't have a lot of time right now to answer them all."

"Harry told me a little about this drug sting that you both are a part of. Veronica doesn't know any more about it than I do, so it's news to both of us."

"I have so much to tell you, Diane. There's so much you need to understand about why I got involved."

"I've been here for you for a long time, Peter, and wonder why you couldn't tell me any of this before."

"I was undercover. I couldn't talk about it."

"We were going to be married, Peter—going to share everything, and you promised to keep no secrets from me. You know how strongly I feel about that."

"We are still going to be married, and this was my last job for the FBI. I'm out of all of it from now on, and I'll be back home to you shortly."

There was silence on the phone.

"Diane? Are you still there?"

"I'm here, and I don't know if we are going to be married. I'm hurt and shocked that you put both our lives in danger. Didn't you think I had the right to know what our future was going to be like?"

"You're upset, and I understand that, Diane. I will have to play this sting out for a few more days, maybe a week, then I can come home to you and explain everything. You have to believe that I love you more than anything, and I want you to be my wife. Nothing has changed for me—nothing."

"But everything has changed for me, Peter. I'll wait for you, but I can't promise we will continue on as before. You see, I'm being honest with you, and it's more than you've been with me."

"I have to hang up now. I love you, darling."

She heard the dial tone and stared for a long time at the telephone in her hand.

Peter sat in the private office of the district attorney and also listened to the dial tone. His stomach lurched, and he felt sick. He realized how much he had hurt her, but he couldn't do anything about it right now.

Diane had cried enough tears in the last week to last a lifetime. She decided to drop by the store and see Veronica. One look told Veronica how much her friend was hurting, so she suggested taking a ride in her car and talking. Susan could handle the customers for a few hours.

They drove to a coffee shop that was quiet at that time of day, and both ordered cranberry-orange muffins and hazelnut-flavored coffee, quick comfort food, and sat at a table in the back.

"Was Peter able to explain anything to you when he called?" asked Veronica.

"All I heard was broken promises. Everything that I hate and despise—all the lies and deceit, that's what I heard. My head and heart hurt, and I don't know what to do anymore." She started to cry.

"Harry told me that Peter went out on a limb to see that this drug operation was shut down for good and that he did it to protect you and your future lives together."

"I understand that, but why couldn't he just have been honest with me? He didn't have to tell me everything, just enough to let me know what I was getting into."

"But he couldn't do that, Diane. He couldn't risk it. Look, if it were me in your place, I would feel exactly the same. But I know that Peter loves you more than life itself, and he would never, *ever* put your life in danger."

She looked down at her coffee cup. "But he did just that when he agreed to take this undercover job."

Veronica reached over for her friend's hand. "Can't you find it in your heart to give him the benefit of the doubt? Can't you put aside your anger and your past life with Carl and cut Peter some slack? Sure, he disappointed you, but his reasons are valid, and you will never find another man who loves you like he does, Diane."

The two women were silent as the waitress came over to refill their coffee cups.

"Peter is an Italian-American, and family means more to them than anything," said Veronica. "His brother died a sad death, and he was powerless to prevent it. He would never be able to rest until he felt he could avenge it in his own way. That tells me he's pretty terrific . . . foolish maybe, but brave and true."

Diane looked up. "Would Harry ever do anything like that?"

Veronica thought a moment. "His sense of justice is as strong as Peter's. He would go after someone who harmed the person he loved—definitely. If you remember, he's saved my life on more than one occasion *and* yours as well. And if it makes you feel any better, Harry does not share the assignments he works on with me. I never know the details. He only gives me what he can or what he feels I need to know. So you see, I'm in pretty much in the same situation as you are now."

They were silent for a while. Then Veronica continued.

"I think you need to get beyond your hurt and welcome Peter home with open arms. Life will be better for you both if you do, Diane. Your future depends on it. Besides, I've bought my bridesmaid's dress now, and I want to wear it."

Chapter 41

The emergency room at the Danvers Memorial Hospital was unusually quiet, and the staff was able to tend to Benny's wound almost immediately. Patricia sat in the waiting room, trying to concoct a story in her mind that would tie in for their records and the police report. She decided to say that she was cleaning her gun and didn't realize the safety catch was off. That would have to do for the time being.

A nurse came out of a tiny office and beckoned to Patricia to sit down while filling out the paperwork. Yes, Benny had health insurance through her restaurant, and, no, he had no other family that could be notified.

The attending ER physician came in to say that he removed the bullet and that the patient was lucky that he only sustained a flesh wound.

"I understand my patient is a chef, and he is right-handed. Let me say that if that bullet had entered slightly to the left, the story would have been quite different."

"May I ask if Mr. Dalton will have the use of his right arm and hand, Doctor?"

"Yes, he will, but he has lost a lot of blood. I'm going to

admit him overnight and monitor his progress for at least one more day. Then I'll reevaluate at that time."

"May I see him now?"

"I'm afraid not. He is drugged and has been given a transfusion and is now resting. He will be moved to a private room shortly. Call us tomorrow for an update. He should be cleared to receive visitors by then."

As Patricia was preparing to leave to drive back to Poppies, Karen ran into the emergency waiting room. She saw Patricia and rushed over to her.

"How is Benny, Patricia? Is he going to be all right? What did the doctors say?"

Patricia raised her eyebrows and could see the distress Karen was feeling.

"Benny is going to be all right, Karen. He accidentally sustained a wound, and they are keeping him overnight for observation. The doctor told me he could be back to work soon."

"Oh, thank God," she said and sank down in a chair. "I was so worried about him when I realized he had been shot."

"Who told you he was shot?"

"Everyone in the kitchen heard the gun go off, and when they told me, I called the police."

"What? I didn't give you permission to call or tell anyone. You had no right to go over my head and do such a thing. It's nobody's business what goes on in my restaurant."

Karen couldn't believe that Patricia was carrying on like this.

"Look, Benny is my friend, my very good friend, and a serious attempt has already been made on his life. I'm not about to let something like this slip by and be hushed up."

"It was an accident, as I told you," yelled Patricia. "I was cleaning the pistol I kept in my desk drawer for protection and forgot that the safety catch wasn't on. The gun went off while Benny was standing right there. That's all there is to it." Patricia was fuming now. "What did the police say?"

"They're sending a squad car down with officers to investigate. We had better get back to Poppies now and talk to them, don't you think?"

Patricia scowled, picked up her pocketbook from the floor, and swept out of the waiting room with Karen following closely behind.

Chapter 42

The squad car was already in the parking lot when the two women arrived back at Poppies. Patricia led the two police officers to her office and closed the door.

"I'm sorry you had to come all the way over here for just a silly accident, Officer," she began.

Lieutenant Balducci took out his warrant card and showed it to her and introduced his sergeant.

"I've been here before, ma'am, if you remember, in connection with the death of your husband."

"Oh yes, of course, Lieutenant. How stupid of me. I do remember you now."

"What I'd like, ma'am, is your version of what happened here today." He opened his notebook and waited for her to begin.

"It will all be in the hospital report, but I was here in the office with my head chef, Benny Dalton. I was sitting at my desk cleaning the gun that I keep for protection in my top drawer. I wasn't aware that the safety catch was off, and my finger slipped. I accidentally fired, and Mr. Dalton, Benny, unfortunately, was standing right about there and was shot."

"I take it you have a license to carry this firearm, ma'am?"

"Oh yes, Lieutenant. I have it right here." She handed him the paper for his inspection.

He looked it over. "It seems to be current and in order," he said and handed it back to her. "Why were you showing Mr. Dalton a gun in the first place?"

"I wanted him to know that it was here if he would ever need it."

"I see. Do you keep the door locked or open when you're not in this room?"

"I keep the office locked even when I'm working in here, Lieutenant. As you can see, my late husband had the door covered in baize to soundproof the room from the noises of the kitchen. It helps to have a place to come to during the day. It keeps me sane sometimes to just stay here for a short time and relax. Do you understand?"

"Yes, I understand your need for peace and quiet. But what I don't understand is why the gun you were holding to clean was positioned high enough to enter Mr. Dalton's shoulder. It seems that you had to be pointing it at him from your seated position. He's over six feet tall. It appears you were deliberately aiming at him."

"No, no," spluttered Patricia. "That's not right. Ask Benny. He'll tell you it didn't happen that way."

"I intend to do just that. I suggest you don't leave the area, and I'll be back tomorrow to speak with you again."

He closed his notebook, and the two men left the office, shutting the door behind them. Patricia remained in her seat, wondering just how difficult it would be to get out of the corner she had just painted herself into.

Karen was prepping vegetables when the two policemen came back into the kitchen area. They briefly questioned her, José, and the two other workers. José showed them the bucket that the bloody towels were soaking in, and Karen gave her version of the story.

The two policemen went back to the station with a clearer picture of the events of the day.

An hour later, the phone in the office rang, startling Patricia from her thoughts.

"Hello?"

"Are you alone, Mrs. Vickers, and able to take this call?" asked a man's voice with authority.

"Yes," she answered. "Who is this?"

"I'm calling on behalf of Mr. S. He has asked me to tell you that he may not be able to communicate with you for a while and wanted you to know he was aware of the two phone calls you made to his residence."

"What does he want me to do?"

"There will be no more fish deliveries for now. You are to proceed as if nothing different has happened. Continue to submit your restaurant invoices to the office to be paid. Do not phone his house again under any circumstances. Your discretion is mandatory, and he has authorized you to deal with things as you see fit. You will receive another phone call from me in a week at this same time. Are there any questions?"

"I have lots of questions but understand your instructions. I want no trouble."

"Do as we ask, and there will be no trouble. Goodbye."

The phone went dead in her hand.

She sat at her desk, deep in thought. Something has happened, and Aldo can't help me. Did the authorities arrest him? He has cut me out just like Robert did, and now, I have to handle things on my own . . . yet again.

She sighed, walked out to the kitchen, and decided to make dough for her special apple turnovers. She always did her best thinking while baking.

Chapter 43

Veronica was tired when she finally arrived home. She was heartsick about Peter's arrest and Diane's refusal to accept that he had acted selflessly. Harry called to invite her to dinner at his house on Beacon Hill. He employed a chef, and it was just as well because she was in no mood to cook. She took a quick shower and dressed comfortably in a black cashmere turtleneck sweater and black wool pants. Her choice of color matched her mood.

Her only concession to fashion, even though her outfit was chic, was to wear a pair of scatter pins made of yellow gold and diamonds in the shape of little bees on her shoulder. Her 1960s-era gold bangle bracelet studded with tiny diamonds and a pair of plain gold hoop earrings completed her look. Since Harry lived a few streets over from her apartment, she decided to walk through the Public Gardens and up Beacon Hill. The early evening cool breeze helped propel her as she thought about helping her friends through their current crises.

Harry's brownstone was brightly lit. She smiled when she saw the pretty vine wreath with fall leaves and flowers hanging on the front door that she had ordered from a popular flower shop on Newbury Street. She slipped her key into the lock, entered the hallway, and hung up her coat. Harry was in the living room reading the paper and listening to Vivaldi on the stereo. He rose and kissed her and handed her a glass of wine.

The room was beautiful, painted a pale yellow and furnished with family antique furniture covered in cream damask. The walls were hung with pictures painted by French Impressionists, many of which were borrowed from the Hunt Collection. Veronica always felt as if she were in a garden when she sat in this room.

"I'm glad you chose to listen to 'Spring.' I sure need to be uplifted this evening, Harry," she said. "What is Chef making us for dinner?"

"I told him to surprise us, but it smells like Beef Bourguignon."

"Mmm. He will have an appreciative audience in me. I just want to concentrate on us tonight and forget about all the turmoil swirling around this week."

The phone rang on the side table next to the bar, and Harry answered it. He listened wordlessly while Veronica stared into the fire that was roaring in the fireplace. The flames glowed red and yellow and mesmerized her. "Thank you for letting me know, Lieutenant," he said and put down the receiver.

He walked over and sat next to Veronica on the sofa.

"That was Balducci on the phone. It appears that Benny Dalton has been checked into the hospital as the victim of a shooting accident."

"Oh no," cried Veronica. "Is he all right? What happened?"

"He received a shoulder wound from a gun fired by Patricia Vickers at the restaurant earlier today. She maintains she was cleaning the pistol she keeps locked in her desk drawer for protection, and Benny happened to be standing in front of her when it went off."

Veronica didn't know whether to laugh or cry.

"There's more," he said.

"Balducci interviewed her personally, and from the angle of the bullet from her seated position, she had to have been aiming it at Benny deliberately. She told Karen Little, who had arrived at the restaurant shortly afterward, that Benny had sustained a knife wound.

"Patricia then changed her story when Balducci interviewed her after Karen called the police. But Karen found the gun on the floor of her office and had the presence of mind not to pick it up. The kitchen staff confirmed that they heard a single shot fired coming from the direction of the office.

"He's going to interview Benny at the hospital tomorrow morning," Harry continued, "and get his side of the story. Patricia has been banned from visiting him there."

Veronica shook her head. "The poor guy has been shot at, and an attempt has been made to strangle him. No wonder he isn't always in the best of moods. I'm glad Karen is there for him, or at least, I think she is."

"I thought you said Benny was sweet on Patricia Vickers?"

"Such an old-fashioned term, Harry, but, yes, I think he was at one time. But now, I believe Karen is first in his affections."

"And what are you basing your supposition on, my sweetie—woman's intuition again?"

"Don't tease me, Harry Hunt. You know very well from experience that I'll put my woman's intuition up against your male supposition any day—and win!"

Just then, the dinner gong went off.

"Saved by the bell," he laughed, and they walked into the dining room to eat.

Chapter 44

Peter rang the doorbell to Diane's apartment. She opened it without a word, and he followed her to the living room and sat down. When he tried to embrace her, she pushed him away. He knew it would be awkward, but he expected a little more warmth than she was exhibiting.

"Diane, I'm not here to apologize. I'm here to explain. Can you at least listen to me with an open mind while I tell you what I've just been through?"

"What about what *I've* been going through, Peter, not knowing what happened to you or whether you were dead or alive? If it weren't for Harry filling me in on some of the events, I wouldn't know a thing."

"Listen to what I'm going to say, and you can be the judge, okay?"

She folded her hands on her lap, and he started his story from the beginning. It took about fifteen minutes to recount.

"That's it in a nutshell. Do you have any questions?"

"I can't believe you put your life in jeopardy like that and didn't tell me. I know," she said quickly, cutting him off, "I know you couldn't divulge any details. I get that. In fact,

Ronnie told me pretty much the same thing about Harry when he goes undercover. He won't give her any details either, and I think it's so unfair."

"Yes, it's unfair, but it's done to protect you, don't you understand? If those drug dealers knew you had information, how long do you think it would take them before they got to you? I had to play along because the FBI and the DEA had to break up a large ring that was operating right under their noses here in Bromfield."

"I know all that, Peter, and I know you did this to vindicate your brother's death. I'm not blind to the fact that you've carried the burden all this time. You've always felt that you alone could stop him from taking drugs, but you must know the decision was his and his alone, and there was nothing more that you could have done to save him."

Peter's eyes filled up. Then the tears started to roll down his cheeks.

Diane reached over and pulled him to her, stroking his hair. "I know, darling, I know. Just let it go. I'm here now," she whispered. "Diane's here now."

Presently, she said, "Veronica says she is helpless to do anything for Harry when he goes undercover and knowing that has made me realize that the loved ones of law enforcement officers suffer right along with the victims of the crimes."

"I know I have a lot to answer for, Diane, but I've resigned, and they can't get me to work for them again. We are going to have our life together and move on. I want that more than anything."

"What about the crew of the *Amanda Jane?* What will happen to them?"

Peter blew his nose loudly.

"You sound like the foghorn on your boat."

He smiled then but quickly became serious again.

"They've all been arrested. That's the worst part for me. But they knew what they were doing, and I had to recruit them. They trusted me, and really, betraying them was the hardest thing I've had to do. They all have families, some with young children, and I betrayed them."

"Peter, what choice did you have? You had to follow orders and think about how many lives will be saved because you did. You have to look at the situation in that light."

"If I can do or say anything to lessen their sentences, I will testify in their defense. But they will all have police records now that will affect their lives forever."

"Will they get their jobs back when they have served their sentences?"

"I can speak to some of the other captains I know and see what I can do to help them. I plan to talk to every one of my crew and explain my circumstances and tell them I'll help them get work again. I have to make this right for them."

"What about making it right for *us,* Peter? Will you retire, or do you still want to go to sea?"

"Right now, I don't know. The only thing I know is that I want to marry you more than anything else in the world."

Diane sat still for a long while. The look of expectation on Peter's face was breaking her heart. She still wasn't satisfied with the situation. Perhaps she never would be, but she knew she loved this man more than anything and would be miserable without him in her life.

"Well . . ." she said finally. "Well, I guess I'll just have to learn how to become an Italian-American wife by proxy. It won't be easy for me, and you'll have to cut me some slack now and then, just as I will have to do the same for you—starting right now."

They fell into each other's arms and made up for the lost time.

Chapter 45

Karen was allowed to visit Benny in his private hospital room for a short time. He was happy to see her, and she smuggled in some bread pudding that she had made that morning.

"This is really good. I like that you use a lot of nutmeg in the recipe."

"It's not too overpowering, is it? And I whipped the cream with just a hint of maple syrup along with the vanilla."

"No, it's perfect." He started to laugh.

"What?" she asked.

"We sound like a couple of chefs, don't we? Anyway, I doubt Patricia could make a dessert better than this. Thanks for bringing it in."

"You're welcome. And speaking of Patricia, what's going to happen to her? Will you bring charges against her for shooting you?"

He wiped his mouth with a napkin and put the empty bowl on the tray in front of him.

"I don't know what to do, Karen. She deliberately shot me, then lied about it to you and the police. She was wrong, and she knew it, and it puts me in an awkward position. If she's arrested, what happens to my job and the restaurant? What happens to your job, for that matter?"

There was a knock on the partially open door, and Lieutenant Balducci walked in.

"I couldn't help but overhear your conversation, Mr. Dalton, Miss Little. I'm here to take your statement, and the doctor said not to tire you out."

"I guess that's my cue to leave, Benny. I'll be back later and bring you something else that's good to eat. I don't imagine the food here is too good."

"They sure could use us in the kitchen," laughed Benny. "Thanks again, and I'll see you later."

Balducci pulled up a chair and sat down. "That's a very nice woman, Mr. Dalton," he said, as his eyes followed Karen out of the room. "Are you close friends?"

Benny smiled. "I know what you're asking, Lieutenant. All I'll say is that I hope we become closer friends in the future."

"Right you are, sir. By the way, how are you feeling?"

"I'm sore as hell, and they're giving me pain pills regularly. I don't like to take the damned things, but right now, I really need them."

"I had a word with your doctor, and he says he will discharge you tomorrow, if all goes well."

"That's news to me, and I'm glad to hear it. I won't be able to cook for a couple of weeks, but the question is, will I have a job to go back to when I'm healed?"

"I would say it all depends on what you're able to tell me now."

Benny recounted his side of the story, and the lieutenant jotted down his answers in his notebook.

"Well, it appears that Mrs. Vickers deliberately shot you. There's no question about that. The question you have to answer is, are you prepared to press charges against her?"

"No, Lieutenant, the question I have to answer is, am I prepared to tell you what I know about her part in drug dealing in Bromfield."

Balducci's eyebrows shot up. "Well, Mr. Dalton, you go right ahead. I'm all ears."

Benny put his head back on the pillow and told the lieutenant all he knew. When he finished, he was exhausted.

Balducci closed his notebook and stood up. "I will have a statement typed up and come back later to have you sign it. I'm going now because you look tired."

Just then, the doctor came in. "Are you finished, Lieutenant? My patient needs his rest."

"Just leaving, Doctor. I'll see you later, Mr. Dalton, and thanks for your help."

He left the room to the sound of steady snoring.

Chapter 46

When Patricia arrived back at the restaurant, she gathered her staff together and told them that Benny would not be returning to work for several weeks. To Karen's great surprise, Patricia asked her to step in to replace him temporarily, and the prep cook was also asked to step up and cover. To the remainder of the staff, she assured them that things would return to normal starting immediately, and if anyone had a problem, they should see her now.

She realized that she had escaped a close shave, one entirely of her making, and she wished that Aldo were here to advise her. The phone call she received letting her know that she could still pay the bills and run things as she had always done gave her some comfort. She also realized that things would deteriorate rapidly if Benny decided to press charges.

She figured that if he intended to hold her accountable, he probably would have done so before now, so it was best to proceed as if nothing had happened. She looked at the week's schedule and saw a full calendar. There was the Andrews-Parelli wedding luncheon to prepare for tomorrow, and she checked the supplies and advised Karen of the menu. She would have to start the wedding cake today but first phoned Diane to assure her that her event was covered, even though Chef Dalton would not be in charge. It was business as usual at Poppies.

———◦◦◦———

Diane called Veronica during her lunch hour to tell her that all was well with Peter.

"We had a serious talk, Ronnie, and I took your excellent advice and forgave him. I realize that life without Peter is not an option for me, and he feels the same, so the wedding tomorrow is still on."

"Then what are you doing working the day before your wedding?"

"I'm a nervous wreck. I need to be doing something, and I just got a phone call from Patricia Vickers. She told me about the accident with Benny Dalton and assured me that Karen Little and her staff would handle the cooking of my wedding meal. Were you aware that Benny had been shot?"

"Yes, Diane, I was. Harry told me, but I didn't want to mention it to you and add more anxiety to an already very anxious friend."

"I have no idea about the details. All I do know is that there will be good food and drink available for my guests tomorrow. I'm glad now that I changed my mind about a cruise for our honeymoon, Ronnie. I think we both have had enough of ships and the ocean right now. Our flight leaves at 3:00 tomorrow afternoon from Logan Airport, and I can't wait to sit on the white sand beaches of Nassau with my new husband."

"It sounds wonderful, Diane. Is there anything you can think of that I can do for you today?"

"No, I don't think so. You said you would pick up my bouquet in the morning, and the florist will deliver the table flowers directly to Poppies. I just hope Peter doesn't misplace the beautiful diamond wedding band you sold him. I can't wait to wear it."

"Your best friend commands you to go home now and rest. You don't want to look frazzled on your big day. Harry will meet us half an hour before the ceremony at the justice of the peace's office, and I will see you at your apartment. If you think of anything else, let me know; otherwise, I'll see you in the morning."

Veronica hung up the phone just as she started to experience the well-known shivers down her spine. Her second sight was telling her to beware.

Chapter 47

Patricia arrived at home that night exhausted from her busy day. She realized she had made a good choice in appointing Karen to take over Benny's place in the kitchen. The woman seemed up to the task, and her relaxed manner translated to the help who were depressed and anxious about Benny.

The phone rang, and she answered it.

"Hello?"

"I have a message for you from Mr. Silvio," said the voice. She sat down heavily on a chair.

"Where is he, and can I speak to him personally?"

"That is not possible, but he requires you to perform a little task in return for his continued patronage and support of you and your restaurant."

"Yes, of course. Anything I can do. He knows that."

"Listen very carefully. He expects you to carry out his wishes to the letter."

The voice outlined a carefully thought-out plan, one that she was sure she could accomplish within the required time frame.

"I will call you tomorrow night at this time for a report."

"I understand," she said. "It will be done exactly as he wishes."

The dial tone sounded very loud in her ear. She undressed and got into bed. Sleep came quickly and deeply.

———◦———

The morning was crisp and cool, but when the sun came out, it felt warmer than it actually was. Harry picked up Veronica at her apartment, and they drove north to Bromfield, stopping first at the florist to pick up Diane's bouquet and Peter's lapel flower and then to Diane's apartment. The plan was that Veronica would help Diane dress, and they would drive directly to the justice of the peace in her car. Diane wanted to adhere to the time-honored tradition of the groom not seeing the bride before the ceremony.

"Do you think I'm being silly, Ronnie?"

Veronica zipped up Diane's dress and helped her into the matching jacket. "Absolutely not. I always think the old ways are best, especially for weddings."

"I guess I'm just superstitious. After everything we've been through, I just want to ensure we have all the luck we need. If Peter saw me before the wedding, he might change his mind."

Veronica laughed heartily. "No chance of that, Diane. You two are going to live happily ever after, as it should be."

Diane had bought a pretty cream-colored hat with a little veil to match her cream sheath dress and jacket. She wore her mother's pearls and tiny pearl earrings but decided against gloves.

"I'm not going to wear anything that will cover up this gorgeous ring. I just can't stop looking at it."

They gazed in the mirror together again, then both reached for hankies.

"You look beautiful, Diane," sniffed Veronica.

"Now, don't let me smudge my mascara, Veronica Howard. I don't want to look like a chipmunk for my new husband."

They laughed and walked out the door.

The drive to the justice of the peace took about ten minutes, and when they arrived, Peter couldn't take his eyes off Diane.

"I had to convince Peter that you weren't going to make a run for it, Diane," said Harry, kissing her cheek in welcome.

"Fat chance, big guy," she laughed. "This marriage is going to take place, no matter what."

Harry gazed at Veronica and smiled. She was a vision in lavender silk and matching turban.

A handful of guests had gathered, and the justice looked at his wristwatch. "I think it's time to begin."

The short ceremony went without interruption, and when he told the groom he could kiss his bride, Peter grabbed Diane with such passion that he almost knocked her hat off.

Everyone laughed and clapped, and they proceeded to Poppies for the wedding breakfast.

Chapter 48

The private dining room was beautifully decorated, and the small wedding party and their friends sat down to enjoy their mimosa cocktails. There were bottles of Prosecco on the tables. "It's never too early to drink good wine," said Peter, happiness radiating from his perpetually suntanned face.

Harry stood up to give his speech. "As best man, I've been asked to say a few words about the newly married couple, Mr. and Mrs. Peter Parelli. I admit I haven't known Peter for a long time but very early on he impressed me with his dedication, loyalty, commitment, and steadfast love for a woman who is bound and determined to keep him on the straight and narrow, whether he wants it or not."

The laughter was loud, and everyone clapped.

"We all know that this is not the first trip down the aisle for this couple. However, it is the last time, and they are both aware that they have been lucky enough to be given a second chance at happiness.

"Diane has finally found the love of her life, and we are all thrilled for her. Naturally, she was reluctant to take him on at first. She wondered what life would be like with a man who gifted her with a box of chocolates and a tin of caviar, both on the same day. But we all know that Peter is a true son of the sea. And in my book, being a son of the sea is infinitely better than being a son of a gun, any day."

The laughter and the catcalls finally died down.

"All that remains now is to toast the new bride and groom. They are here today because they love each other and were meant to be a couple. We celebrate them and their future life together because we believe, as they do, that love conquers all. Let us raise our glasses and toast: To Diane and Peter."

Harry sat down to applause, and Veronica leaned over and kissed him. "What a beautiful speech. One would think you were a romantic man, Harry Hunt."

He kissed her back and gazed into her eyes. "Did you ever doubt it, Veronica Howard?"

The waitstaff started to serve, and the rest of the meal went without interruption. When the wedding cake was brought in, Patricia went over to Peter and Diane and congratulated them, and graciously accepted their thanks for her creation. Peter was especially complimentary and raved about the recipe.

"I have a sweet tooth, Mrs. Vickers, and I can honestly say this is the best cake I've ever tasted."

She smiled, shook his hand, and thanked him before going back to the kitchen.

The celebration lasted until early afternoon, and after all the wedding guests left, Harry and Veronica stayed behind as they were driving the couple to the airport.

"I'm a happy man, Harry. I can't believe I'm so happy,"

said Peter when the two men were alone together at the table.

"Before the ladies return from the powder room, I want to thank you again for your part in Silvio's arrest. By helping to put him away, I'm finally at peace and content. I'll never have to work for him again, and he will never be able to get to me now."

A waiter approached the table and said that Mrs. Vickers wanted to speak to Peter alone in the kitchen. She had a bottle of wine to toast his wedding with, and if he followed, she would give it to him personally.

Peter smiled, got up, and followed him just as Diane and Veronica returned to the table. Harry explained that Peter would be right back.

Patricia greeted Peter as he tentatively stepped into the busy kitchen.

"Oh, Mr. Parelli, here you are," said Patricia. "I want to give you a little remembrance of your wedding meal here and to thank you for your kind compliments on my cake. Just come down with me now to the wine cellar, and I'll choose a nice vintage for you."

Peter followed her down into the basement and shivered involuntarily.

"Sorry for the chill," she said, "but the room is climate controlled for the wine." She led him over to a table that was set up with three wine bottles and glasses.

"I've chosen these for you to choose from. Take a look and tell me which is to your taste."

Peter leaned over while taking his eyeglasses from his jacket pocket. "You're so generous to do this, Mrs. Vickers. I'll need some input about what you suggest."

He peered intently at the labels and picked up a bottle to examine it.

Peter didn't hear the thud of the heavy object connecting forcefully with the back of his head. He went down on the flagstone floor like a dejected rag doll. He also didn't feel his body being dragged over to the bottom of the staircase and couldn't hear Patricia's labored breathing from her exertion.

He didn't feel her pushing him and arranging his body artfully, and he didn't hear the crash of the wine bottle on the floor next to him.

He didn't feel or hear anything because he was no longer alive . . .

Patricia gave one last look around then ran back up the stairs hesitating in the doorway to the kitchen, swaying back and forth while grabbing the doorjamb. Karen happened to look up at that moment and saw her.

"Patricia, are you feeling all right? You look ill."

"There's been an accident," she cried. "The man I was with tripped on the stairs and fell. He's not moving."

Karen ran over and led Patricia to the office and sat her down. "Do you want me to call an ambulance?" she asked.

Patricia started to shake. "Bring his wife in here. I'll speak to her. She's the bride we served today."

Karen ran out, found Diane, and told her to come immediately, that there had been an accident. Veronica and Harry quickly followed her into the office.

"Patricia, what's wrong?" cried Diane. "Where's Peter . . . Where's my husband?"

Patricia was crying now and pointing to the doorway. "I took him downstairs," she choked. "I took him down so he could choose a bottle of wine from the cellar as a gift for your wedding, and he tripped on the stairs."

"Where, where?" yelled Diane, running through the now-quiet kitchen with Harry and Veronica following closely behind.

Patricia took them to the cellar door. Harry reached out and stopped Diane from going down the stairs.

"Veronica, take Diane back to the office."

Diane was hysterical now, yelling Peter's name.

"Come on, Diane," said Veronica. "Let Harry help Peter first. Come on. That's right."

She took Diane's arm and guided her back to the office.

Harry ran down the stairs and immediately noticed the broken glass surrounding Peter's body on the floor. He saw a roll of plastic wrap on one of the tables and tore off two pieces to cover his hands before examining the head wound. He checked for a pulse. There was none. He slowly stepped back and wiped away the tear that was starting to run down his face with his wrist.

He looked around and walked over to the table with two wine bottles. They were placed in a row, side by side. He started to shiver and returned upstairs.

Patricia had joined Veronica and Diane on the office couch, and they all looked up expectantly when Harry walked in. He walked over to Diane, knelt down, and took her hands gently in his.

"He's gone, Diane," Harry whispered. "We've lost him."

"No, no, no, no," she wailed. "You're wrong, Harry. He's not dead. Let me go to him. He needs me now." She started to get up, then collapsed against Harry.

Harry glanced at Veronica, and it broke her heart. It was a look of hopelessness, pathos, and anger, all in one.

She leaned over to take his place and held a sobbing Diane while he telephoned the police.

Chapter 49

Lieutenant Balducci asked his officers to clear the restaurant after taking all the diners' names before they left. The kitchen staff was being interviewed individually, and it was evident that none of them had observed the accident. Even Karen was unaware of what had taken place until she saw Patricia in the doorway.

Veronica accompanied Diane home to her apartment after the medical examiner gave her a strong sedative. A police car drove them, and Harry stayed behind to provide his statement.

Balducci was sitting with Harry and Patricia in her office, and she was telling her story again.

"I'll never forgive myself, Lieutenant, for suggesting that Mr. Parelli come down to my wine cellar and choose a bottle of wine. I only wanted to gift him with a commemorative bottle, especially after he graciously complimented me on the wedding cake I made for them."

She sat at her desk weeping gently into a hanky.

"Tell me again, ma'am, when you realized that Mr. Parelli had fallen."

She looked up quickly. "I heard him—I mean—he tripped and fell heavily on the floor. I was walking ahead of him, and I heard him fall."

Balducci looked at Harry. "Let's all go downstairs, and you can show me."

Patricia got up from the desk and led them down the cellar stairs. She pointed to the bottom step. The crime officers had chalked the floor around Peter's corpse before the medical examiner had removed the body for the post mortem.

Balducci walked around the stairs, taking note of the placement of the end of the railing. Harry stood to the side, listening.

"Tell me again the sequence of events."

"As I told you, Lieutenant, we were at the table here looking at the bottles."

"Did he choose a particular bottle?"

"He did ask me to suggest which one I would choose."

"It appears that he took your recommendation, picked up the bottle, and walked away with it. By the way, which wine was it?"

"Pardon me?"

"Which wine did you recommend?"

"I told him I liked the Lambrusco."

Harry walked over to one of the crime scene officers and asked him for the evidence bag containing the bottle fragments. He glanced at the bag, then handed it to Balducci.

"It seems he preferred the Pinot Grigio. Here's the label still intact."

"Is that somehow significant, Lieutenant?" said Patricia.

"I'm just trying to understand what happened here, ma'am."

"Of course, forgive me. I'm still in shock that such a freak accident could happen in my restaurant."

"That's understandable, ma'am. My officers will be here for several more hours. Would you like to rest awhile in your office? I noticed that you have a sleep sofa there."

"I would appreciate that, Lieutenant. I need to telephone some of my patrons who have reservations for tonight and tell them the restaurant will be closed for another day or two, at least. Will that be enough time for you to investigate further?"

"That should do it, Mrs. Vickers. If not, I'll keep you informed."

Patricia walked back upstairs, and Balducci took his sergeant aside. "Watch her like a hawk, Anderson. I want to know who she calls and who calls her."

"I'm on it, Lieutenant. We're bugging her house phone as we speak, and the office has already been taken care of."

Harry walked around the cellar, now in his mode as an investigative law officer. His grief put aside for the moment, he was looking at the wine racks with a critical eye.

"There are a lot of nice vintages down here, some very expensive wine."

Balducci followed Harry around, and they noticed a small, refrigerated unit in a dark corner. He opened the lid and glanced at the contents of a frozen joint of meat along with some sausages and chops. Harry closed the lid, and they continued over to a desk that had a large leather diary on it.

Balducci opened the book, leafed through the pages of

the wine inventory, and whistled. "Some of these bottles cost a hundred bucks apiece. I could drink a week's salary worth in just a few minutes."

"Something's nagging me, Lieutenant," said Harry. "I know Peter was exceptionally sure-footed. After all, the man was captain of a fishing boat. He was used to rolling seas, and his excellent balance was a tool of his trade. How then could he trip on a stair that was a step or two up from the floor and hit his head with such force that it would kill him? Something here just doesn't make sense."

"I see what you mean, Mr. Hunt. Accidents do happen. But I'm inclined to agree that the scene we are looking at is very fishy, if you'll pardon the pun."

He reached into his jacket pocket and extracted a licorice stick. "Do you know if the victim was right-handed?"

"I happen to know he was left-handed," said Harry. "Peter always wore his watch on his right hand the way that lefties always do. Today, for some reason, he didn't wear a wristwatch. I know what you're thinking. So why was the bottle broken on his right-hand side if he was walking up the stairs with the wine in his left hand?"

"Good question," said Balducci, chewing thoughtfully. "My guess is that she hits him with something heavy, drags his body over to the bottom of the stairs, then smashes the bottle to make it look like he tripped on the stairs. Only she didn't realize he was left-handed. Let's wait to see what the pathologist says. Maybe I can speed up the autopsy report."

Chapter 50

Karen drove Benny home from the hospital and made them some coffee.

"Oh, Benny, it was awful. That poor man, married only a few hours before he had a fatal accident. I'm trying to process in my head how someone can die because they tripped on one step."

She sipped her coffee and continued speaking as much to herself as to him.

"Patricia said she had given him a bottle of wine as a gift, and then he somehow slipped and hit his head on the stairs or the floor."

Benny was quiet for a long time.

"Can I get you anything?" she asked him presently.

"No, I'm fine, Karen. I was just thinking how bad luck seems to follow Patricia Vickers around. First, her husband's body is found in the restaurant, and then I am seriously attacked. Next, she deliberately shoots me, and now a customer has a 'fatal' accident, also at the restaurant, and all within the space of a few months.

"I'm a firm believer in making your own luck, though.

I see the whole thing as a house of cards that started to fall when Robert decided to act like a jerk, and she decided to go along with it. Things have spun out of control, and I suspect Patricia now has blood on her hands."

"Do you think the police realize it?"

"I'm sure they do. I've never known her to gift a patron with a bottle of anything. That sounds completely out of character for her. You know how Patricia holds on to her wines like they were her children."

"Yes, I know what you mean."

The doorbell rang, and Karen went to answer it. Lieutenant Balducci walked into the room.

"I see you're well enough to have been discharged, sir. I thought I would take the opportunity to ask you a few more questions before you got too tired. And I'll speak to Miss Little as well, seeing that she's here."

"Ask away, Lieutenant."

"I'm sure you've heard about the events at Poppies. Can you tell me anything about the wine cellar? Does Mrs. Vickers handle the wine and liquor herself?"

"Yes. I cook wine reductions all the time, but Patricia handles the liquor ordering and storing, now that she no longer employs a full-time sommelier. I've been down the cellar a few times, but she prefers that I leave the details to her."

"Does she usually give bottles of wine to patrons?"

"No, she doesn't. Karen and I were just talking about that. I've never known her to do it. In fact, she keeps the keys to the cellar in her office, locked in her desk drawer."

"How about you, miss? Have you had an occasion to access the wine?"

"No, Lieutenant. It's as Benny says . . . that's Patricia's private domain."

"The cellar only houses wine?"

"Yes. It is climate controlled and represents a large investment. Robert was a connoisseur and very fussy about his cellar."

"What about the small freezer case down there?"

Benny and Karen looked at each other.

"That's just there for the vodka, Lieutenant, which needs to be served chilled. That and the Akvavit. Robert had a thing for those drinks, and I believe he kept the case there for his personal use when he worked down in the basement."

After Balducci left, Karen stayed with Benny, and they watched television for a while until he started to get drowsy.

"Sorry to be a party pooper, Karen, but I can't keep my eyes open."

"I'll leave you now to rest. I'm still wondering why Patricia would give a bottle of wine to a patron. I can't imagine her doing that, can you?"

But Benny had fallen asleep and couldn't answer her question. She let herself out of the apartment but couldn't stop thinking about the day's events and why she was questioning Patricia's behavior.

Chapter 51

The autopsy report arrived at Balducci's office the next morning while Harry was there. It was delivered personally by the medical examiner.

"Thanks for bringing it over so quickly, Ed. This is Special Agent Harry Hunt of the FBI, who knew the victim. Let's see now: 'blunt trauma to the head with a heavy object,' he read from the sheet while reaching for a stick of licorice from the canister on his desk.

"Still eating the licorice, Phil?" asked the medical examiner.

"Just trying to keep on the straight and narrow."

"Whatever works. You'll notice that the wound was deep and slightly curved and not at all consistent with the edge of either the step or the stair railing, not to mention the floor."

"We searched the area thoroughly after it happened and couldn't find any item that fits this description. According to the prime suspect, the victim tripped on the first step and hit his head."

"Wait a minute, Lieutenant," said Harry. "We may have overlooked something important here. I'm thinking about a murder weapon that Patricia Vickers could have used that was hidden in plain sight. This may be a stretch, but would a frozen leg of lamb be able to deliver a blow that could cause death?"

The medical examiner scratched his head. "If she hit him with considerable force, I don't see why not."

"That would fit, and the joint of meat we saw in the case would have the curved edge consistent with the wound," said Balducci.

He quickly reached for the phone. "Anderson, take a squad car over to Poppies Restaurant now, go down to the wine cellar, and bring back the leg of lamb from the freezer in an evidence bag before it thaws."

Chapter 52

Patricia arrived home with a sheaf of papers and a large tote bag. She declined the policeman's offer of a ride and instead, drove her own car. The first thing she did when she walked in the door was to turn on the oven. She then placed a phone call to someone she was always comfortable with.

About an hour later, Mrs. Violet Thompson arrived with cleaning supplies.

"Thank you for coming over on such short notice, Violet, but I need you to clean up some of this mess."

Violet looked around and couldn't understand why she had been called. She had only been to the house two days before to clean, and nothing looked out of place to her. She suspected that the real reason she was there was that Patricia wanted someone to keep her company. The woman really looked exhausted.

"Just do some light cleaning, and if you have the time, perhaps you'll join me for dinner."

She didn't need to be asked twice. The delicious smells coming from the oven made her mouth water. Since Kevin's death, Violet hadn't really had much of an appetite. She realized she needed the company just as much as Patricia Vickers did.

About an hour later, they sat down to a wonderful meal of roast lamb with mint jelly, a fresh vegetable medley, and oven-baked potatoes. Violet smacked her lips and thanked her hostess profusely.

"I haven't enjoyed a meal so much in a long time. You never met my Kevin, but he only liked plain food, especially his mother's cooking. Now, of course, I don't have him to cook for any longer."

"I'm sorry for your loss, Violet. I know what it feels like to lose someone."

Violet wiped away a tear. "He wasn't perfect, but he was my son. The police tried to tell me he was dealing drugs. Can you imagine that? No, Kevin would never stoop so low as to associate with any horrible lowlife that pushed drugs."

Patricia looked hard at her and said nothing. She wondered if Kevin ever discussed their association. She would have to find out just how much Violet knew.

"There are plenty of leftovers, so why don't you take the rest of this food home? No, Violet, I insist you take it all. I'm really so tired now. Could you clean up the kitchen for me before you go? I'm going to turn in early tonight. Just lock the door on your way out."

Chapter 53

When Sergeant Anderson arrived back at the station empty-handed, events started to move quickly. A squad car arrived at the Vickers house, and Patricia was asked to accompany the officers to give a statement.

"I've already told you all the information I can, Lieutenant. Why am I here?"

"Just a few points that we need clarification on, ma'am," explained Balducci.

"I'm so tired and haven't been sleeping well, as you can imagine. Can we make this fast? I need to take care of a lot of paperwork in anticipation of the restaurant opening for business again."

Balducci referred to the file folder in front of him and extracted a piece of paper, examining it carefully. "Tell me why you wanted to gift Mr. Parelli with a bottle of wine."

"I've already explained that to you several times, Lieutenant. It was a gesture to thank him for both his business and for his profuse compliments on the wedding cake I baked for him."

"Have you given other patrons a wine gift?"

"Once in a while, I do, but not often."

Balducci referred to the paper again. "Why didn't you just hand Mr. Parelli a bottle instead of asking him to go down to your wine cellar?"

"I just thought I'd make a grand gesture, I guess. Poppies has a fully-stocked cellar that few patrons are even aware of. He was quite impressed, which is what I wanted."

"I see. By the way, what happened to the joint of meat that was in your basement freezer yesterday?"

Patricia said nothing for about ten seconds. "Do you mean the leg of lamb?"

"Yes, that's the one."

"Why, I was saving it to take home to cook, which I did."

"You're telling me that you removed an item from a crime scene, ma'am?"

"I took my dinner home to cook last night, Lieutenant, which couldn't possibly be the same thing."

The door opened, and Sergeant Anderson beckoned to Balducci. He got up from his desk, and they had a whispered conversation in the doorway, then he returned to his seat.

"You couldn't have eaten the whole thing yourself. What did you do with the leftovers?"

"I had a guest for dinner and gave it to her to take home."

"May I have the name of the guest?"

"Of course. Mrs. Violet Thompson, my cleaning lady," said Patricia triumphantly. "Are we finished here, Lieutenant?"

Balducci scowled and returned to his report. "Who supplies you with the fish for your restaurant?"

Patricia was caught off guard. "Well, I, er, let me see. Oh yes, that would be the Santa Flavia Fisheries in Gloucester."

"Have you been doing business with them for a while?"

"Yes. My late husband was responsible for the contact. They do a good job for us."

"Are you aware that the owner, Aldo Silvio, is in FBI custody for being the kingpin of a major illegal drug operation in the New England area?"

Patricia was speechless. "I, no, I didn't know that. I've never met the man."

"Well, that's not quite true, is it, ma'am? We are aware that you have been in personal and telephone contact with Mr. Silvio for quite some time. We know that one of his shell companies has been responsible for paying your restaurant's invoices and that he has visited you there on several occasions."

"I want to talk to my lawyer before I say anything else," she cried.

"That can be arranged, ma'am. From what I can see, you *will* need representation."

Chapter 54

Veronica had been staying with Diane at her request since the day Peter died. Her friend had cried, and now the next step in her grief was anger. She couldn't understand why she had been singled out for all the bad luck in her life.

"What have I done to deserve this pain, Ronnie? I was on the threshold for a wonderful life with a wonderful guy, and now this."

"You must console yourself that he was a man who did the right thing, Diane. No matter what Peter was about, he did the right thing. He wouldn't rest until Silvio was behind bars for good, and he gave his life for his convictions."

"But he left me alone, Ronnie. I'm all alone once again."

The apartment doorbell rang, and Veronica was surprised to see Harry standing there. He came in and sat down across from the women.

"I have some news. I've just come from Lieutenant Balducci's office, and the case has been blown wide open.

"I don't know how else to tell you this, Diane, so I'll just blurt it out. Peter was murdered by a stone-cold killer."

"I told him not to work for that damned drug baron. I

knew it would end badly."

"It was Aldo Silvio who ordered Peter's murder, but it was Patricia Vickers who carried out those orders."

"What? It can't be! She looked me in the eye. She arranged for our wedding celebration, and she baked my wedding cake . . . She wished us the best!

Harry went over and put his arms around her. "That's what stone-cold killers do, Diane. They use every trick in the book to get what they want, and she was under orders to kill Peter for retaliation. He knew too much about the drug operation, and when he turned state's evidence, he signed his own death warrant."

"Did she confess, Harry? Is that what this is all about?" said Veronica.

"Yes, she did. She spoke regularly to Silvio. He was paying the restaurant's bills in return for her part in accepting shipments of fish that contained packets of cocaine. She distributed the drugs to selected dealers who met with her at Poppies after hours. She also admitted that Aldo Silvio was her lover.

"We also now know that Silvio ordered Benny Dalton's beating and Kevin Thompson's death. Kevin was dealing drugs and beginning to get sloppy and brag, but Benny had nothing to do with any of this business. His assault was ordered to send a message to the others to keep them in line. He was innocent in all of this. Patricia was in too deep to get out, and she would have done anything to keep Poppies going."

"She sold her soul for her restaurant, didn't she, Harry?" said Veronica.

"She told Balducci that her husband had let her down with his gambling and drug habit, and she wasn't going let that ruin what they had built together. Silvio was the way out for her, and she willingly went along with whatever he wanted to keep her business going."

"It didn't matter who got in the way, and my Peter got in her way," cried Diane. "May she rot in hell for all eternity for what she did to him—and to us!"

"It's a good thing she confessed because we had very little proof that she murdered Peter. The circumstantial evidence showed that he couldn't have slipped on the stairs like she said because the wine bottle was broken from the wrong hand. She struck him down with a frozen leg of lamb that she had placed in a freezer case that her husband used for his vodka. She admitted to doing this the day before your wedding breakfast, so her actions were premeditated.

"Patricia was very cunning, though," continued Harry. "She took the lamb out of the case and cooked it for dinner that night. Then she invited the unsuspecting Violet Thompson over to help her eat it and insisted she take the leftovers home. The thrifty Violet carved the rest of the meat from the bone to make a stew and threw the bone away."

"Poor Mrs. Thompson," said Veronica. "When she realizes that she was eating dinner with the woman who hired her son to deal drugs and was responsible in arranging to have Kevin murdered, she will be devastated."

"She has already given Patricia Vickers the Irish curse of never having another happy moment for the rest of this life and into the next."

"And I'll add the Sicilian curse in Peter's name that the devil takes her for his own."

"I think that's already happened, Diane," said Veronica.

Chapter 55

A few days later, Karen Little stopped into Veronica's Vintage. She was smiling and happy.

"It's nice to see you, Karen. What can I do for you today?"

"I wonder if you can show me that nice diamond ring in there," she said, pointing to a box in the showcase.

"It would be my pleasure." She took the ring from the box and placed it on a black velvet pad.

Karen picked it up and put it on her left-hand ring finger. The gesture was not lost on Veronica.

"It's so beautiful. When was it made?"

"This is from the Edwardian Era, so from 1901 to 1910. It's made of white gold, and the diamond is an old mine-cut stone of a little more than one carat. The two small side stones are rubies. I have to say it looks very elegant on your finger."

"My hands are small, and I don't like large rings. This does look nice, doesn't it?"

"May I ask if this is a feel-good present, or would it represent a deeper meaning?"

Karen's face flushed a deep shade of pink. "Well, you will

find out soon enough, so I'll tell you now. Benny proposed to me last night, and I said yes.

"Congratulations, Karen! I wasn't aware that you and Benny were an item."

"We have known each other for a while and only just recently realized we have so much in common. He's a wonderful guy, and I'm crazy about him. He told me to pick out a ring that I liked and suggested I consult you about it. I saw this in the showcase the day I came in. Oh, I just remembered. That was the day I met Patricia here, and she offered me the job at Poppies.

"That seems such a long time ago now, but I'm sure it isn't."

"So much has happened since then. Benny and I fell in love, and we have decided to buy Poppies when it goes up for sale. I understand Patricia will need the money to pay her legal fees."

"What a wonderful idea, Karen, but will you be able to afford the asking price?"

"It's not generally known, Veronica, but Benny and I come from wealthy families. We both decided to go our own way without their money, something else that we have in common. So, yes, we will be able to purchase the restaurant. We have great ideas for it going forward and now I have this lovely ring that I love, and he will have something special to place on my finger."

The words Karen was saying reminded Veronica of Diane . . . similar words she uttered not so long ago. A lot had taken place recently: lives that had been lived, lives that had ended, lives in mortal danger, and now love and marriage again. The rhythm and the continuous circle of life and death were always present. You have to live, and you have to die, and in between, there is love.

Today, there was love, and Veronica was ready to celebrate it.

CPSIA information can be obtained
at www.ICGtesting.com
Printed in the USA
LVHW090407281021
701751LV00001B/125